FIC
TRA
TRACY

What do cowboys like?

DATE DUE			

WHAT DO COWBOYS LIKE?

Ann Tracy

THE PERMANENT PRESS
Sag Harbor, New York 11963

Library of Congress Cataloging-in-Publication Data

Tracy, Ann Blaisdell.
  What do cowboys like? / by Ann Tracy.
      p.   cm.
    ISBN 1-877946-52-4 : $22.00
    1. Teenage girls—Maine—Fiction. 2. Love stories—
Authorship—Fiction. I. Title.
PS3570.R26W48 1995
813'.54—dc20   94-20260
                                                                      CIP

first edition, January, 1995

Manufactured in the United States of America

THE PERMANENT PRESS
Noyac Road
Sag Harbor, NY 11963

CHAPTER ONE

I don't want you to think that I'd never been in love before. It was just that this time it all seemed so much more possible.

My last attack of love (a year and a half earlier, when I was fifteen) had clocked an 8 on the Richter scale but only about an 0.2 on the Possibility scale. However, what being in love with Ray Bradeen, who was too old to notice me much and was dating my senior friend Jillian besides, lacked in possibilities, it made up for in obsession. Mainly I was fixated on his name and spent the spring of 1956 stealthily covering up words and pieces of words—the "Bradbury" on a Ray Bradbury book jacket, the "O-Vac" on my Ray-O-Vac flashlight—to produce tiny declarations all over the house, little hur-*ray*s for love. The only other thing I did about this non-affair was paint a picture of a skinny brunette girl, me, Louisa Fisher, in a bedroom walled with books, drooping melancholy on the windowsill while a couple who look a lot like Ray and Jillian walk past, hand in hand. ("Hello," the girl is calling silently; "Turn your gorgeous face to my window and rescue me from Dickens and Charlotte Brontë and the Book-of-the-Month Club. I could be a princess!")

The organdy curtains were the most technically impressive feature of the painting, I thought; you could see right through them. My mother, who could usually see right through me, did not hesitate to point out other resemblances to real life. "Nice picture of Ray and Jillian," she said, smirking. "And I suppose that's meant to be you?" I left the room.

I don't remember how I slid into that obsession with Ray, but my more possible love just sort of dawned on me all at once, as though it had perhaps been getting ready for a while and I hadn't noticed it. Maybe it had been, because Dwight Brown and I had been friends for three years (he was a boarder, I a day student), ran with the same crowd, and plain out liked each other. I thought that was all. Maybe he hadn't registered as romantic because he was only my own age, or only my own height (short), or somewhat less suave than Rhett Butler (I'd read *Gone With the Wind* more than once), though quite a lot nicer. His being a boarder lent him a certain glamour, though. In a little town like ours, anyone or anything from AWAY was valuable for its assurance that the world really reached beyond what we could see: one general store, two churches, a restaurant, fifty million trees, and a big sky—not enough to satisfy the spirit of adventure. The names of other students' towns, no matter that they might be as wanting as our own, had a kind of music. Stetson, Stillwater, Sedgwick, Easton, Solon, Winslow, Ilseboro, Jackman. Sweet elsewhere.

So there I was, walking down the sidewalk past the school on a Saturday morning, watching the leaves zag down, and sucking up the cold Maine air, and there before me was Dwight, nailing a football rally sign to a telephone pole. All of a sudden I was so glad to see him that I wanted to yell and sing and chase the leaves over the rooftops. I compacted this new and alarming impulse into one subtle hop that I figured he wouldn't notice.

"Hi, Dwight," I said, staring straight into those cerulean blue eyes, glad my slacks were pressed. Original stuff.

"Hi. Fish," he said. "I'm nailing up this poster."

"It's a nice one," I said, stunned by love, basking in his smile. "Did you make it yourself?"

"Oh well, thanks," he said, blushing a little, "but you're the real artist."

"Aw," I said, more eloquent by the minute.

How could we both be so shuffle-footed and tongue-tied when my heart seemed to be trying flips and barrel rolls with its new wings? Life and literature were parting company fast. I could imagine it, my golden moment, preserved in a ballad:

There was a maiden loved a lad

Was nailing up a poster;
"Young man," quoth she, "did you
make it yourself?"
Shuffle, Blush, Shuffle,
"It's a very nice one!"

Hey nonny, terrific.

But of course it really was terrific, though I joked about it, one of life's milestone mornings.

Dwight's nail was nailed. I stood there a minute longer, staring hard at the poster, trying to nail the moment too. Dwight shuffled a little longer and then he left. I didn't mind being alone, though, because I wanted to get acquainted with my new state. "Dwight, Dwight, Dwight," my acrobatic heart caroled as I danced to the post office, blessing the unmailed letters without which this amazing revelation might never have happened. "How strange," I said to myself over and over, "that suddenly after three years you should be in love with Dwight Brown, but how perfectly right."

Dwight, of course, was still gone when I came back, but his poster was there and I memorized every line he'd drawn (a Canterbury Academy knight sinking, with his lance, a battleship full of the other football team), straining to discover the hieroglyphics of love. Even the sight of the telephone pole had a certain sentimental impact. I touched its splintery gray surface with a furtive and loving hand. Sun warmed, it seemed to arch its back under my touch. I leaned against it and pretended to shake a pebble out of my loafer. I would have liked to linger on that spot, but at sixteen you never hear the last of a pole fetish.

Bound for my room now, I sailed past my father, who was raking and offered to share the fun ("Thanks, Dad, but I wouldn't want to horn in"), past my mother, who forgave me for forgetting her stamped postcards but looked at me with too much speculation ("No, honestly, Mom, nobody special"), past my little brother Herbie, who was making poison crystals in a saucepan ("We cook food in that, Lamebrain"). All three were bathed in the spillover of love and looked unusually huggable, but I wanted solitude, with nobody looking into my eyes to surprise my secret. The peace of my own place began to touch me as soon as I started up the front stairs into the quiet, sunny landing that led to the front of the house.

As always, my room was as soothing as Noxema on a sunburn, a thick, cool, second skin that kept me safe. There if I wasted time dreaming, as I often did, nobody noticed. There if I sketched, no kindly interest looked over my shoulder. There if I wept, nobody saw my face. I didn't know how people with no private space survived the vulnerability of adolescence; perhaps they used other kinds of walls. One friend told me that her diabolical parents, instead of sending her to her room, forbade her to go to it, forced her to stand all unshelled in the fire of a family quarrel.

My room told me, if I was in danger of forgetting, who I was or wanted to be. The walls were papered with birch trees on a white background (''Hall paper, but suit yourself,'' my mother had said) and the woodwork was not white, as it was everywhere else in the house, but pale green. These aberrations proved that I had elbowed myself some space, had an impact on environment. My chenille bedspread was cherry red, a bold stroke with the green and white. Objects were carefully, though perhaps not tidily, arranged to make a statement. Some of the statement was not altogether true. For instance, there was a tennis racket and a can of balls in the corner, though I rarely played tennis, and then not well. But I had not yet gotten past thinking of myself as someone who did. And I had them ready for what I can only describe as the invisible Life Inspector, that unknown observer who might suddenly pop up and interview me for *Time* or make notes towards a biography, and look favorably upon the well-roundedness of a tennis racket. I really did use the box of oil paints under the window, and the bookcase was, except for the bed, the most important object in the room.

A lot of the books were my own, an odd assortment bought with hoarded allowances—*Great Tales of Terror and the Supernatural, A Time to Love and a Time to Die, Peyton Place*. Other favorites had been abducted from

the family collection. On top of the bookcase, pictures
of my friends sat like icons, telling the Life Inspector
and me what I loved most. Viv and Sabra, my dearest
and best. Jillian, who'd graduated and now wrote
scrawly, thought-provoking letters from the University
of Maine. Bonnie, whose parents had carried her away
to Kansas.

I lay on my back and stared at the ceiling fixture.
Dwight. I invited the thought of him into my sanctuary
and reviewed past kindnesses. That night in our freshman spring when the trees were green as glass outside
the window and I was wearing my black skirt with the
gondolas on it; we were practicing for public speaking
and he'd bought me a popsicle from the study hall ven-
dor. The French II test when I'd panicked and cried, "I
can't remember the word for *lost*" and he'd said out
loud, "It's the name of a university, Fish," and started
singing the Purdue song and taken his scolding. And how
he had lingered, how we both had lingered, over the
embraces required of our characters in the Junior play.
Why hadn't I known then that I loved him? It had all
been building up like the iceberg that took the unsinkable
Titanic. And though I was not willing to ski downhill or
take my feet off the bottom of the lake to swim, I planned
to yield myself to the glittering iceberg force of love and
plunge below the surface to see the marvels of the deep.
Though of course it hadn't worked out too well for the
Titanic. Perhaps a different image.

I turned my head to the right. Through my eastern windows, from which I could see the horizon covered now with trees like flame, I was accustomed to look with longing, thinking of the Atlantic washing up against the coast a hundred miles away, and beyond that Paris, Venice, the stuff of dreams. Today the horizon was enough. Just *try* to get me out of town.

Outside the third window, behind my head, the road ran south to Portland, Boston, New York, to art museums and bookstores and things happening. I yearned for the wonders of Harvard's university museum, which my mother had told me about, its glass flowers and bottled babies. I wanted to drop my quarters in the slots of a New York Automat. I dreamed of a season in Greenwich Village. In summer, when all Canterbury's boarding students had gone, the aching for experience could drive me night after night to pace and stare out the screen door south into the blackness. Not even the stars looked as far away as New York. The school blocked the horizon in that direction, but today the school was as far as I cared to look, for tonight the focus of all longing would lie there under those stars on his school cot.

I sighed with pleasure and fingered my dreams. What did I want? What could I get? Dwight had moved to the top of the list: I wanted him to love me back, and I wanted to know it for sure. I had liked the looks of his embarrassment, but that was not hard evidence. This fulfillment seemed possible, for loving him was already as sweet and soothing as a cashmere sweater. (A theoretical analogy—I didn't have one.) I wanted, nay planned, to be valedictorian of my class, and to write a best-selling novel before I was twenty, while the reviewers would still call me a prodigy. I saw no problem there. My most cankering, though intermittent, desire was for freedom. I knew that I had a good life—a home that smelled of flowers and baking, new clothes twice a year, hardly any housework and only one sibling. But, oh, my parents hemmed me in with their very love, their interest. My father's rules, my mother's friendly curiosity. I wanted to be grown up and never again ask permission or hide my mail or dodge a question or guard new passion with averted eyes. I wanted out from under the good life. In that fall of my senior year, escape seemed not possible at all.

CHAPTER TWO

Of course I went to the rally that night. If Dwight's poster, sentimental as I felt about it, had announced a picnic in hell I'd have been making sandwiches without mayonnaise so they wouldn't spoil in the heat. More important, I figured I'd see him there, and then anything could happen. The stars were out. Everybody knows that romantic things happen in starlight, right? And to be honest, I would have gone to the rally anyway, because I was trying hard to be a passably normal teenager, and teenagers are known to like rallies. My friends seemed to like them well enough. I hadn't so far gotten the hang of them, though. Maybe this one. The fact is, I was embarrassed by all the jumping and hollering, and doubly embarrassed because I couldn't bring myself to do it. I deplored that release of animal spirits; I would, by preference, have sloughed my body like a snakeskin and walked as pure spirit. And yet there was no denying that

I felt a social outcast because I couldn't unlock my mouth and let out a partisan bellow. Life could be most unsatisfactory.

What's worse, I really did love that school. It was the only thing of any importance in our town, and I'd waited all my life to be old enough to go to it. I would gladly have genuflected to it or sacrificed a heifer to it or maybe tattooed its initials on my forehead, but I just couldn't holler about it, and that made me feel disloyal on top of everything else. However, guilt was one more push rallywards.

I didn't rush over, though. I'd think of Dwight and itch to start, but then I'd think of the screaming crowd and read one more page of the *Saturday Evening Post*. When I finally slid into my jacket and headed out the side door, my mother winked at me. "Good hunting," she said. Evidently I hadn't gotten my face past her fast enough that afternoon. Brooding on the horrible accuracy of her perceptions, I skulked over the fallen leaves and frosty grass, willing myself invisible, sneaking up on the bonfire from the back, even my hands gone shy and hiding in my jacket pockets.

Too soon I came to the edge of the firelight, where I stood and peered at the savage forms leaping around the flames. Who would imagine that they had ever sat in rows and solved quadratic equations? I was sorry that

Viv and Sabra were, as usual, away for the weekend. If they were with me they'd either yank me into the crowd or ease my loneliness by staying out of it themselves. They'd know how much hollering was enough and how to do it without looking like fools.

Finally I saw Dwight on the other side of the fire. He was throwing some broken boards onto the flames with a glad cry as the sparks went up. Dwight too could be normal without being silly. He hadn't seen me yet. I was almost ready to sneak away again and forget it, but I still wanted him to know that I'd responded to the poster in some fashion, that I'd come because *he* urged it. I began to edge around the perimeter of the firelight, just casual drifting, one foot accidentally coming down a little farther to the right each time I moved it. Hiya, Dwight, here I come. I gabbled a little poetry to myself to steady my nerves and confirm my skill at *something*—"Ah distinctly I reMEMber it was in the bleak DeCEMber and each separate dying EMber wrought its ghost upon the floor. VAINLY I had sought to borrow from my books surcease of sorrow . . ."

"Hey, Fish," Dwight's voice said beside me. I jumped, beamed, felt a sense of safe harbor.

"Hey, Dwight," I said, and dropped anchor.

"I didn't see you here," he said. (Aha, had he been looking?) "I thought maybe you hadn't come."

"Of course I came," I said, "after that nice poster. I saw you. You were throwing some boards on."

"Yeah?" he said. Was he wondering if I'd been looking for him too? He leaned companionably against my right shoulder. "It's a pretty good fire," he added, "if I do say so."

"An excellent fire," I agreed, thinking many thoughts and trying to express passion with the outer muscles of my upper arm alone.

We stood there for some tongue-tied and blissful moments, while the bloodthirsty shouts of our peers seemed to grow more harmonious. But that kind of in-between state can't last. Either you have to talk or you have to fall into one another's arms in earnest. Dwight straightened up. "What time is it?" he said. "I have to meet Spence at nine." And with a quick one-armed shoulder hug he was off again into the darkness. Soon after that I went home, not because I minded the rally any longer, but because I'd had more or less what I'd come for. There was no point in staying.

My mother looked up when I came in. "Rally over already?" she asked.

"Pretty much," I said, "and I got chilly."

"Go take a hot bath and rub your chest with Vicks," she said. So I did. It was easier to do it than to argue.

I was more eager than ever for Monday, though that may sound perverse. I hadn't seen Dwight again that weekend, except for a glimpse of him at church, where he sat on the far side of somebody bigger. But Mondays always brought my world back together, for they gave me the context I was good at, and better yet, they brought my sweet friends back safe from their weekends, their other lives.

Let me pause for a moment to tell you about Viv and Sabra, how cool and soft and clean they were, how able to rise to any occasion, how confident. Their sweaters and skirts never wrinkled, their hair was always shiny, their skins never broke out. They had romance covered. Viv had been dating the same boy for three years and was going to marry him. Sabra had dated dozens, and one summer had successfully gone steady with two boys at once, switching rings and pictures as one left and the other arrived. Viv was practical, blunt, cheeky, down-to-earth, but vulnerable. Sabra was unflappable, haloed with luck—obstacles melted from her path as she approached. "Butterfly," "Honeycomb"—all the songs were about Sabra.

Viv and Sabra seemed to know, in those home-ridden 1950s, all about how to manage the households that they would surely have, for they had taken Home Economics along with their academic subjects, as I had not. It was at their suggestion that we three chose our silver patterns and gave one another spoons or forks or knives for Christmas and birthdays. (My hope chest so far contained two forks, a beach towel, and a Japanese nut bowl. I had never dared to ask about theirs.) Now and then they would grill me on domestic topics.

"Okay," Sabra would say without preamble, "you

just got married and had chicken for dinner. What will
you make with the leftovers on the second night?''

In my eagerness to prove myself, it would never occur
to me until afterwards how unlikely I was to cook on my
wedding night. ''Salad!'' I'd say, ''I'd give him chicken
salad! Or maybe soup!''

''That's right,'' Viv would say, ''but how do you
make chicken soup?''

Two pairs of well-loved eyes would narrow at me as
I gibbered about hot water and celery. Two flawless
faces would look at one another and then back at me.
Two brushed heads would nod approval. I had passed
again.

But I knew in my heart that I was a marginal pass at
best, in a world preoccupied with love and marriage.
Some days I was pretty, some days I wasn't. My hair
wouldn't stay parted. The writing callus on my middle
finger was dyed with ink. My clothes were good, bought
at the same stores as Viv's and Sabra's, but standing
alone in the middle of a room I would wrinkle and
smudge. My sneakers came untied in the spring. In the
fall my penny loafers shed pennies like copper leaves.
I sniffled all winter and my pockets bulged with wet
handkerchiefs. To be sure, I had some areas of mastery.
I could get my lipstick on straight and blot off the excess.
I could walk on high heels and not fall over. I could
sleep on curlers and not toss. But I was full of secret

flaws. I wore Windsong cologne, for instance, not because I cared about the scent one way or the other, but because I liked the free sound of the name. O Wild West Wind. I recognized that this was not the right motive.

I did not tell Viv and Sabra that I was in love. Not just because they would have scolded and laughed and stepped up the instructions for making chicken chow mein, but because volunteering information about the inside of my head honestly never occurred to me. They would have found my head furnished with all the wrong things—elephant-foot umbrella stands, say, where I should have had dinette sets. In fact, Viv and Sabra didn't tell me much about themselves either, though when I got one alone she quite often told me interesting things about the other.

Of course some silences were the outward signs of tact and affection. For instance, I never told them that their eleventh-grade pancake makeup, which ended abruptly at the jawline, looked like orange masks. They in turn did not mention to me that my tenth-grade trick of camouflaging pimples with snippets of flesh-colored Band-Aids was more grotesque than the pimples themselves. I did not very often point out that certain of their boyfriends were scumbags. They almost never let me know quite how hopelessly out of it they thought I was. Perhaps they were more candid with each other, for they were roommates and shared the freedom of the outside world as well. I belonged only to the school part of their lives, but I belonged to it hard and would have welcomed a chance to kill for them. Their friendship buoyed and flattered me.

There was one other thing that I was keeping from them on this particular Monday, as well, though I think that they would have been both pleased and encouraging had I told them. I had decided, over the weekend, to start my first novel. I had originally planned to put it off until I'd seen more of life, but my moment with Dwight by the telephone pole had suggested what seemed to me an important truth, that the exterior circumstances of life weren't much to look at and if I wanted to achieve greatness I'd have to help life along, supply events important enough to match emotions. I thought about this as I sat behind Viv in study hall, gazing absently at the extraordinary whiteness of her neck between her blue sweater and the feathery ends of her dark hair. If I scrubbed my neck all day and all night I'd still be swarthy. Sabra, across the aisle, was all attention to Taylor Hoffmann, the quarterback, who was evidently giving her some interesting signals.

How pleased they'd be with me, Viv and Sabra, when I pulled out the finished typescript like the king of rabbits. Dwight's friendly face would glow too; did people fall in love with authors much? If I told them now, before it was done, would Viv say, "All right, but how do you *make* a novel?" In my house, as big a problem as making it would be keeping it private, something on a par with concealing a pregnancy.

Viv swung around in her seat. "Is there something wrong with the back of my head?" she hissed. "I can feel you staring at it."

"No, no," I whispered. "Sorry, I was just thinking."

"Well think about math then," she said. "Have you got the answer to number eight?"

I put down *Les Miserables*, took out my math book, and lost myself in abstract calculation. This did nothing to reconcile me to reality, though it did reinforce my notion that you can represent anything with the right symbol. As soon as I finished, I poked Viv in the back.

"$A^2 + B^2 = 4$," I said. "You missed the rally."

"Big deal," she said.

I surmised that things had not gone well with her fiancé that weekend. Likely Sabra would fill me in if she got a chance.

Dwight and I had exchanged the briefest of greetings between classes, and that was all. Now he was sitting four rows to my right and one seat ahead. I could watch him, though not easily. Perhaps if I willed it very hard, he'd turn and smile at me. I squinted my eyes, except for a bit of my right eye, which I kept trained on Dwight's shirt collar. Oak desk tops, golden with afternoon sun, blurred and quivered through my lashes. "Dwight, Dwight, DWIGHT," rose my silent scream. "Turn around, see me, SMILE." I kept at this for a long minute or two, but nothing happened except that Viv turned around again.

"Good lord, Fish, have you got a pain or what?" she snapped.

The voice inside me left off screaming and said, "Indeed, madam. The joys of love are but a moment long, the pain of love endures forever." My lips said, "Oh. No. Sorry."

"I don't know what ails you, anyway," Viv said, but she said it with a tinge of affection, enough to keep me content. As for her not knowing, I was more than content with that.

CHAPTER THREE

I was eager to start writing, but I had to wait for a good chance. I hoped to get my typewriter upstairs, at least, before the family questions began. So the week wore away in homework and ball games and television and frustration, but at last, when I came home after school on Friday, I saw my moment. My mother was sitting at the kitchen table with a wire rack of hot chocolate chip cookies and a very old Jehovah's Witness who had just made a mess of his cookie and was gummed up in melted chocolate like a fly in syrup. I knew him. His name was Mr. McGlaughlin. We always let him in and were nice to him, because we did that with people, even the crazy old lady next door, of whom I may say more later. (It was easy to get into my house; getting out of it was the hard part.) When Mr. McGlaughlin would say, "Do you know who the 144 thousand are?" my mother would say, "Yes, all Baptists," and they'd both laugh.

"You know Mr. McGlaughlin," she said now.

"Yes," I said. "Hello. Glad to see you."

He gave me a sad, chocolatey nod.

The sound of gunfire from the living room told me that Herbie was safely occupied with his after-school western. My father wasn't home yet. I had to move fast, though.

I dropped my books, except for the lit anthology, in the dining room and shed my blazer onto the arm of a chair. The typewriter was heavy, not all that portable, but I snatched it up from beside the downstairs desk, swung it around the corner and sprinted with it up to my room, where I gently closed the door to the hall and drew a deep breath. Having taken the typewriter out of its case, I set it on my bedspread and looked at it to see if it might be leaking the words of my masterpiece already. It wasn't, but they would come. My father had bought that typewriter for me the summer before, just given it to me as a surprise. He would have a surprise, too, if he knew what I was going to do with it.

In the lit anthology and the books on my shelves I hoped to find guidance in the art of making real life bigger than life. There was some typing paper in my bureau drawer, stashed in case of sudden furtive bouts of drawing or note writing, but I'd need more.

I began to take things off my dresser, the piece of furniture that most closely resembled a desk. I had just taken away the crocheted doilies and pushed the perfume bottles into the far corners of it when I heard my mother's footsteps coming down the hall. Panicked, I began to sweep the bottles and jars back into the middle. Doilies! Where had I put the doilies?

The problem was, my mother was good to me. She came in my room to vacuum and empty the wastebasket and put clean clothes away, and how can you quarrel with that? Her interest in the details of my life was jolly, open, non-judgmental. Also insatiable. As she knocked and came in with four ironed blouses on hangers I shuffled cosmetics with a wild hand.

"Cleaning my dressing table!" I panted.

"That's nice," she said, not for a minute deceived by so unlikely a story. She rolled her eyes now and then towards the typewriter on the bed. "Maybe you should throw out that bottle of Evening in Paris you've had since sixth grade and never wear."

"I might do that, I just might do that," I lied. I was used to the look of that bottle right where it was—round, blue, reliable.

The door closed behind her. Still panting slightly, I pushed the bottles back again and lowered the typewriter into the cleared space. I moved the lamp so the carriage wouldn't hit it, and I opened the upper right drawer a couple of inches so that I could shove manuscript in with my scarves in a hurry if I had to. Then I rolled in a piece of blank paper, moved my hairbrush off my pillow, and lay down to think about titles. I should have at least—

I'd read the phrase somewhere— a working title. What would cover, or suggest, all the breadth of experience that I hoped to explore? What would encompass the great themes of love, sex, death, and freedom, as well as any other great themes that might come to me later? I flipped through *The Rubaiyat of Omar Khayyám*, handy on the bedside table, hunting potent phrases. *And Naked on the Air of Heaven Ride* by Louisa Fisher. Too racy. *A Box Whose Candle Is the Sun* by Louisa Fisher. Super, but too ambitious even for me, and not very pertinent. I was getting depressed. The combination of Omar Khayyám ("One thing at least is certain— *This* Life flies") and the Friday afternoon exodus from school called up a familiar dread, never far off, that something would happen to my friends. Now and then they'd catch a glimpse of this—"It's stormy! Be careful how you drive!" I'd cry—and then they'd jeer at me and tell me not to be such an old lady. I wasn't fooled. Omar the Tentmaker knew. When I went back to the title selection, oriental gloom, perhaps, colored my choice, but it looked good in the middle of the first page.

ONE MOMENT IN ANNIHILATION'S WASTE
or
Love, Sex, Death, and Freedom
by
Louisa Fisher

I added the subtitle in case the title turned out not to mean anything.

And now, I said to myself, to Re-Mould this sorry Scheme of Things nearer to the Heart's Desire. My fingers touched the keys, but Herbie's knock, lower than my mother's, made me snatch them back. I sprang up, running to open the door first and stand in his line of vision.

"Do you want any cookies?" he asked what he could see of my face through the crack.

"Oh," I said, "that's nice of you, very nice, Herb, but I guess now I'll wait till after supper. I'm doing some stuff here anyway." I suspected that he'd been sent ("Go ask Lou if she wants a cookie and find out what she's up to"), but maybe not.

"I'll be down pretty soon," I said, not opening the door any wider. Herbie wandered off, looking sorry. I was a little sorry too, but an artist sometimes has to be ruthless. I sat back down at the dressing table. Get ready, world. Me and D.H. Lawrence.

Chapter One

Lucilla Shark threw back the blankets and slid from her bed, shivering like a mare at the caress of cold air on her skin. The solitude of the night was hers. In the dark she pulled on her clothes with no more consciousness of her action than some healthy draft animal, her large thoughtful eyes fixed on the darkness outside. She thought it better not to risk a light, but she had left her upper right drawer open when she went to bed, and now she slid her fingers into the opening and groped until they touched paper under her scarves. This she drew out and put, folded, into her skirt pocket, feeling the points of the thumbtacks secreted there already.

She listened to the animal sounds of her—

My father's voice drowned the sounds of Lucilla Shark's world: "Suppertime!" I pulled out the page, stuffed it in the drawer, and went down.

"I'm sorry I didn't realize," I said. "I was writing a letter."

"Lucky you had your typewriter handy," said my mother.

It was Sunday afternoon before I could get back to work on Lucilla Shark, but I'd been thinking about her. I sat at the dresser and willed the autumn sunshine away, called darkness into my mind. I spread my fingers with confidence.

She listened to the animal sounds of her sleeping family, the sweet breathings of her little brother, the unconscious growling snores from the room where her parents lay curled in their familiar dents. Her bare feet, silent on the stairs, brought her to the back door, where she put on her wool socks and loafers and tip-toed out.

Some compulsion too strong to deny drew her on as it drew the orange moon through the murk of the clouds. Steadily, inexorably, she made her way to the dead tree in front of the school, thrusting silver into the moonlight. She was all alone and exultant in the freedom of the nighttime world. She knew what she was going to do. She unfolded her paper and cupped the tacks in her hand. One at a time she drove them fiercely into the tree. Her poster gleamed in the moonlight—

A rap on my door. I jumped. The daylight came back.

"Are you warm enough?" said my mother's voice. I could tell from the sound of it that she was pressing her cheek against the wood, wondering what I was doing.

"I'm fine!" I said. "Plenty warm enough, thanks!" I was in fact shivering, but it wasn't from the cold, it was from the shock of being ripped from one world into the other.

"It's such a nice day," the voice went on, "that we thought we might drive to the fire tower and buy some

apples on the way back. The whole family. Are you too
busy to come?''

"No, oh no, not at all!'' I exclaimed, throwing doilies
on top of the typewriter to hide the paper. She might
give up nuzzling the door and open it at any moment.
"I'll be right down, I'd love to go, you go on ahead and
get ready,'' I babbled.

I heard laughter in her voice as she left, calling down
the stairs, ''Grab your jackets, she's coming!''

Well, nice, I guess, to be wanted. But I decided right
then never to be a pervert. I mean, what do you do if
someone comes in while you're wearing rubber underwear and hitting yourself with a whip? It's hard enough
to cover up a novel. "It's the *mosquitoes*,'' you'd have
to say. "They're so *bad* this year!'' My knees were
shaking a little when I went downstairs, but nobody
commented.

The outing was in fact a pretty good one after all. The
leaves were still in full tilt and I'd taught myself how to
stare at them until the world shimmered and slid away.
I climbed about half way up the tower. Lucilla Shark
would have gone to the top, but more than halfway up
it shook too much for my taste. From there I could see
over rows of hills and feel myself delightfully alone.
(They looked familiar, those little folks on the ground
looked familiar. Had I met them? But they had nothing
to do with me.) Queening it in the tower was like sitting
in the front of the motor boat in summer, making myself

forget that there were people behind me, one of them indeed steering the boat. Solitude, velocity, elevation. Even a Fish in a tank knows some delusive sensations of freedom.

CHAPTER FOUR

After I took my books home on Thursday, I went for a walk alone, hoping that nature would chase certain goblins out of my head, which is funny because I guess in a way the goblins were *about* nature. But scenery was okay—leaves, so smooth and separate; rocks, leading their dry, civil little lives. I felt better as soon as I was away from campus and down by the empty public buildings, like the Baptist church and the Grange Hall, white-clapboarded and silent. I stopped to lean a minute over the cemetery fence, staring at a front-row stone, 1853, on which an ornamental "Miss," spotted with lichen, stood about eight inches taller than the name of the dead woman. Bet there was a story behind that, but nobody remembered it any more.

Had she, like me, wished that people were made out of something more dignified than meat? Would my gravestone say "Miss"? And what was I going to do when I came to the sex part of my novel?

Because, in truth, the whole topic of sex made me fairly nervous. No, not nervous—phobic. My problem went beyond not enjoying the undistinguished grapplings with the boys who walked me home, for I knew that the they, too, were just learning technique. One part of it was my own feelings of monumental ignorance. I dreaded the knowing leers of certain boys younger than I and not generally considered bright, whose specialized knowledge I did not wish to plumb. When anybody told a joke, I tried to sidle out of the room before the punch line, in case it should depend on some double meaning beyond me, in case I should laugh too hard or not enough or in the wrong place, and so give myself away as an ignoramus. When I was younger, thirteen or so, it had taken even less to upset me. I blushed at the very sight or sound of certain unfamiliar words that *might* prove to be lewd—scrofulous, maturation, pedicure.

The newest gall was a vile-sounding question that the boys shouted around the corridors, like half a riddle. How had it gotten to be so important to me? How could it seem so sinister? I didn't even know the answer to it, and I was afraid to find out. The boys knew that, and loved it. "What do cowboys like?" they'd ask each other and crack up at an answer that they all understood and didn't need to voice. Nothing like a silent allusion to make anybody feel like an outsider. But you understand,

and the boys certainly understood, that I wanted to be
inside even less than I wanted to be outside. So if I
leaned out the hall window to look at the autumn, the
question would wing up from the boys' smoker below—
"Hey, Fish, what do cowboys like?" They'd laugh to
see me pull my head back in. Or it would whisper from
the back of the study hall, floating like a malign wraith
to my seat—"Cowboys, what do cowboys like?" I'd
pretend not to hear. They weren't mean to me otherwise,
not at all, and I guess they thought they were just having
fun, but I could feel underneath it some pecking instinct.
Worst, from the steps of the boys' dorm: "Do cowboys
eat fish?" I ignored that one hard. Guess I didn't fool
anybody.

The cowboy question had become the perfect embodi-
ment of my insecurities. The answer to the riddle had to
be sexual, didn't it? I mean, would they make all that
fuss if the answer was "horses"? So the question con-
jured up not only my possible ignorances but the things
that I didn't want, didn't feel ready, to know. By supply-
ing the right answer, I could probably escape this vicious, haunting question. But the question was vicious
and haunting largely because it suggested answers that I
didn't want to give.

The boys never did it, though, when Dwight was
there. If he walked up, the question dissipated and blew
away like bad air, and so did the fear. I could breathe
again. Being with Dwight was like being safe on home

base. With Dwight there, your cuts healed and the rain held off and x always equalled the right answer. If I had to learn cowboy lore, I preferred to learn it from him, but with him I never felt ignorant; I felt that if the answers mattered, they'd be along later. Need I mention that I was still in love?

Loop by loop, my psychic tangles unsnarled themselves as I watched a weed, a tree, a shadow. I picked up a damp, cool white rock by the Grange Hall steps and rolled it in my hand, counting the rusty veins. A car passed. Did the driver notice me, poetic, sensitive, advanced lover of all nature except the birds and the bees? "Every prospect pleases," I told myself, "and only man is vile." And boys are viler. But not Dwight.

I did not ordinarily go farther south than the Grange Hall on my walks, or perhaps into the little field just beyond it. I don't think that I had been forbidden to do so, but some instinct suggested that the last of the public buildings was a natural boundary. My grandmother had told me that she once knew a crazy woman who believed herself to be tied to her house by an invisible rope. It was quite a long rope and let her go to some places but not others. "Why don't you shop at such-and-such, Nell?" the neighbors would ask her. "Can't, rope's not long enough," she'd say. My rope was about a mile long, maybe. Feeling it jerk, I started back up the hill towards school and home.

Imagine my delight at seeing Dwight and Willard Jewell out for a stroll themselves and coming towards me.

I loitered a little at the cemetery fence again, waiting for them, while they picked their way carefully past the stretch where a neighbor's manure spreader had hit some bumps. Ah, the romantic countryside. I would have tried to ignore the grosser parts of life, but it was no use with Willard, who was singing "Tiptoe through the Cowshit" while Dwight cheered him on. We all treasured Willard Jewell's wise-mouth clowning, as good as Jackie Gleason, and if his quick wit suggested to any of us that he had brains he should have been cultivating, we managed to forget it; we needed him just as he was.

Dwight and Willard came across the grass and leaned on either side of me against the cemetery fence. Willard's mouth had changed stations but not stopped broadcasting. "Just out for a stroll through nature's beauties," he said expansively, "the cow—birds, and the cow—slips, and the cow—"

Dwight reached past me and kicked him, giving me a sidelong glance to see whether I was embarrassed. "We saw you out for a walk yourself and thought we'd meet you," he said. I was enormously pleased.

"I used to spend a lot of time in here when I was little," I said. "I liked all those neat verses on the stones, and I used to play hide and seek with the minister's kids."

"Give us a tour, Fish," Dwight suggested, taking my elbow. We walked through the gate three abreast, but Willard, who tended to turn into things, turned into a tour bus driver and began to megaphone through his fist,

"And on your left, under a tasteful marble stone—note the willow design, folks—," and showing off my childhood favorites seemed the wrong tone.

We all flopped down on the grassy sides of the winter tomb and began playing with leaves. I hunted for pure hues, fanning them out like a color wheel. Willard tucked leaves behind his ears, and Dwight lay on his stomach, stripping a leaf down to its veins and looking restless.

"Madame wants a bouquet," he announced suddenly, jumping up on Deacon Phillip Hammond (1869-1912) and launching himself from there onto the lowest branches of a maple. This was better than orchids, for I had observed that boys often climbed things—trees, swing sets, door frames—and hung from them when girls they liked were around. And I was the only girl in sight. When he dropped back to earth with a leaf bouquet in his teeth, some conversational barrier seemed to have been breached, and we began to ask each other questions, casual, even superficial questions, but it wasn't a thing we usually did. We usually knew each other in context, and that was all. After a while it fell into a pattern, like a game.

"What's your father do, Jewell?" I asked, rolling onto my back so as not to disturb Dwight's leaf bouquet in my buttonhole.

"Same thing as these folks," he said, his hand sweeping the cemetery. "He's dead."

"Gosh, I'm sorry," I said. "What happened to him?"

"Bunch of Japs shot him," Willard said, looking unconcerned as hard as he could. "He was in the South Pacific. I was just a kid. But my grandfather—he got run over by a train."

Dwight and I were delighted. "How come?" we chorused.

"He was drunk. Walked onto the track and said, 'You think *you're* big, by holy—' "

We all laughed and rolled in the leaves. Grandfather Jewell, if he'd ever existed, had long since been cleaned off the rails; only the joke of his death was left. He sounded like Willard.

"My turn," said Dwight. "What does Fish do in the summer—fish?"

"Actually, I do fish once in a while," I said, still giggly from Willard's story. "We have this summer cottage up north on Portage Lake. We keep going there, and there's no phone and no mail and nothing to do but stick hooks into worms. I hate it."

I felt a pang of shame as I said this, as though I'd been mean about a family member, someone kind and loveable with embarrassing habits. I hated only part of it—those eternal evenings of lamplit solitaire, the anxiety of wondering whether I'd have mail if I were home, loneliness that drove me to hold my sweatshirt in my arms at night for comfort.

"It doesn't sound so bad," Dwight said kindly. "Just lie back and pull in the dinner, what a life."

"It's boring," I said again, unable to change direction. I thought of the wood smells and water sounds that had put me to sleep every summer of my life. Me on the screen porch, my insteps against the window ledge while I got dizzy from too many hours of cramming down *War and Peace*, and the base of my spine ached against the metal lawn chair. The glass jugs of well water in a row on the bench behind me, water that tasted of confinement and screw-on metal tops. (If Dwight kissed me, would I too taste of confinement?)

It felt strange to be talking about that private, non-school part of my life that none of my boarding friends had seen. I liked the questions very much, especially the fact that none of them were about cowboys. My fingers wove themselves deeper into the cool grass. And here, I said to myself, we are, in our moment above ground, our moment to have longings and secrets and autumn sun. Our moment in annihilation's waste. That title should work okay.

Willard rolled onto his side. "Right, Dwight," he said, "You haven't told us all *your* secrets yet. Now for the sixty-four-dollar-question—"

All at once I felt my face turn pink. Willard might ask anything. Dwight looked appalled too. What was Dwight afraid he'd ask? Could it be something about me? Could it? Ashamed of my blushing, I felt myself turn redder yet. Willard Jewell was looking at us both with interest and compassion. "The sixty-four–dollar question," he said gently, "is don't you think we'd better get Miss Fish home before she's late for supper?"

I wasn't late, I was early, so I ran up to my room to reread the passage I'd managed the night before while Mom was at Ladies' Aid.

> Her poster gleamed in the moonlight—"Death to Cowboys." She felt a wild sense of liberation as she reread its vicious letters.
> All at once she was aware of movement on the other side of the tree. She tensed and felt her bones turn to mud. She put a steadying hand against the rough bark and held her breath. For a moment a figure with a hammer in its hand set her heart racing, but then the familiar and secretly loved features of Brownell Flite resolved into clarity. He gazed at her poster with wonder.
> "I was putting up a poster too," he whispered. They stared into one another's eyes.
> Lucilla sank to her knees in the cold grass, overcome by the pulsing of her blood in her veins. "Do you love me, then?" she whispered painfully.
> In answer Brownell sank down to meet her and warmed her in his arms. "I always have," he murmured.

CHAPTER FIVE

Half a dozen short writing sessions (and some amorous rally scenes) later, my father began to puff up with theory. This had been bound to happen sooner or later. Attacks of theory were almost his only child-rearing flaw, but they were a bad one. He once had, for instance, the idea that when you made a call you should let the number ring only twice, and until the idea wore off he'd hung around the phone barking "That's enough!" when he figured we'd gotten to the third ring. Or he'd decide that Herbie had too many pairs of pants or comic books or whatever. These attacks didn't last long, usually, but they were hard on us. I hated to be jerked around by somebody else's whims. Once at the cottage when I was having cramps and reading, he decided that I was ill from idleness and would feel better if I painted screens. Finally my grandmother came out to help me and in the end the two of us poured the rest of the paint down a hole and told him we'd used it up. I imagine that afterwards I looked to him brighter-eyed, happier, better content; but I wasn't.

Now, Sunday night, sitting at the table eating supper, I realized that I was in for it, that my literary sessions in my room had not gone unnoticed. My father's tone was playful, even benevolent, but not misleading to one who knew him.

"It's a hard thing for a person to have too much time on her hands," he began. "Why, it can lead her to lock herself in her room and forget the light of day." Forget the light of day? For a moment I was startled; had he read my night scene, that he was able to make that all too pertinent remark? But then I knew that he hadn't. Sneak-reading was not his style. "Sometimes a person needs the fun of a little responsibility," he went on.

I could feel my lower lip begin to poke out. Nasty word, responsibility. Sure to be unpleasant. A foreboding tear slid down my nose and splashed onto my tuna mushroom-soup potato-chip casserole. Everyone was kind enough to ignore it. I stared at my plate and swallowed a bite of casserole before it got too salty, for I suspected that the bad news was just beginning.

"Chickens," my father said with satisfaction. For a moment I peered at the casserole, wondering if it was a new recipe, but it tasted like tuna. Nope, he wasn't talking about supper. "Eggs," he went on, "the rewards of industry."

I tried to retreat inside myself and get away from this increasingly ominous conversation. Sometimes I could do that, but not often. I couldn't do it now. I was about to be hauled into something ridiculous, lesson-teaching, humiliating, and smelly. There was no stopping it, or stopping the increasing leak at my eyeballs. Where was the Little Dutch Boy with his thumb when I needed him? Mom and Herbie were listening with wary interest, dry-eyed. They hadn't been spending too much time in their rooms, they were safe.

"We could put about three dozen hens in the back corner of the garage," he planned happily. The back corner of the garage? It was full of cobwebs. *Spider-webs.* SPIDERS! Rather death than spiders!

"Spidery," I whimpered. He rose above it, indeed soared over it without a glance.

"You can feed and water them every day and collect the eggs," he said, "and then you can sell the eggs and you'll see that work pays off. It will get you out of your room and get you some fresh air."

Fresh air, ha! I'd been in henhouses, though not any oftener than I could help. Fresh air, my foot! Ammonia and feathers and feed and hen mites, that's what you breathe in a henhouse. Add cobwebs for the garage, and maybe a little car exhaust. Yummy!

"May I be excused?" I croaked. They let me go, but words not meant for my ears drifted after me up the stairs—*immature, responsibility, Plymouth Rocks, educational.*

In my room I wept and paced behind the closed door. Did any other authors go through this, turned into egg-sellers against their wills? Embarrassing! Smelly! Scary! Boring! Dictatorial! What would my friends say? When Dad saw that I still spent time in my room (because finish the novel I must), would he want to start me raising calves? Why didn't I live in a city, where chickens were zoned against? I'd never had anything against chickens before, but now I hated them with my whole being. Poultry phrases clucked through my mind—chicken out, chicken-hearted, chicken-shit, laid an egg—and none of them were good.

At last I flung myself down on the bed, wrung with emotion, and rubbed my wet cheek on the chenille. I dozed off briefly then, but when I woke up ten minutes later, drooly and dazed, I had an encouraging dream to remember—Dwight, like a pied piper in his band uniform, playing his saxophone and leading a thousand chickens out of town to their deaths.

I went to school on Monday with chickens still roosting in my mind, shuffling their skinny feet and laying no eggs. This was an inner upheaval that I did wish to share with Viv and Sabra, for I needed their supportive indignation. With difficulty I waited until noon break; after all, I didn't want the whole school to know. I spent the morning obsessed, drawing hens in my notebook

margins, hens in Indian costumes dumping eggs into
Boston Harbor, 36 x hens + *As* = 3 dozen dead hens,
Où sont les poules d'antan? A chicken for every aca-
demic pot.

When the bell rang I grabbed my coat and made sure
to intersect Viv and Sabra as they headed to their rooms;
I of course went home to lunch.

"Emergency!" I puffed and caught at Viv's sweater,
noting as I did so that even her internal heating system
was better than mine, for though she always wore lighter
clothes than I and let her coat fly open all winter, she
never caught colds.

She brushed my hand away like lint but I could see in
her face not only coolness but a marshaling of forces. If
I really had a dragon, she was prepared to slay it. Sabra,
on her other side, held her sympathy cocked and ready.

"Now what are you talking about, Fish," Viv said
too firmly for a question. "You've looked all morning
like you'd sat in an ants' nest."

"Nest is the key word," I said, feeling myself grow
hot. "I don't know how to tell you this, but my father
is going to make me raise chickens."

"My lord, chickens," Viv said, looking staggered.
"If that isn't the damndest piece of nonsense I've ever
heard."

"It's the rural factor," Sabra groaned. "My father
brought home an actual lamb he'd gotten from some old
farmer who bought feed from him, and expected me to
raise it with a bottle."

"I didn't know that!" Viv and I chorused, delighted.

"I was too embarrassed to tell anyone," Sabra said. "I was only in seventh grade and I didn't want to be a shepherdess."

"What did you do with it?" I asked, imagining Sabra as the prettiest shepherdess in Arcady.

"I gave it to my little sister. She was too young to take care of it, so it just went away. I suspect we ate it later."

"Gross," Viv and I said absently.

"My brother's too smart to take the chickens," I said, "so what am I going to do?"

By now we were at the girls' dorm, and my friends were anxious to go in and drop their books. They looked at one another and came to some conclusion.

"Restaurant?" Viv asked.

"Three forty-five," Sabra answered.

I began to feel some slight return of exhilaration, absent since supper the night before.

"Look," Viv and Sabra said, "You just meet us at the restaurant at quarter of four. We'll round up the boys and we'll have a council of war. He can't do that to you."

The restaurant, in fact, always made me nervous. It was the place where I was most keenly aware of not being very good at adolescence, aside of course from the acne and tears. Or to put it another way, I was unavoidably doing adolescence, but I was lousy at being a teenager. I thought the music was too loud, though I liked the songs, except the silly ones, and though I rather admired the clouds of cigarette smoke, I found breathing difficult. Furthermore, I was so unresigned to wearing a body that it embarrassed me to fuel it in front of my friends. All these misgivings notwithstanding, I looked forward to the council of war.

My mother looked pleased and interested when she heard where I was going, for I suppose it pained her sociable instincts to see me steering clear of, and I quote, the Teenage Hangout. Any day now, she was probably thinking, my daughter will straighten out and start to put tea cozies in her hope chest.

By hanging back I managed to enter the restaurant at the same time as Sabra and Viv. The boys were holding a booth for us, piled in three on one side, with the other side for us. I was happy to see Dwight there to fight for me, and Willard Jewell. Skinny Marcus Andover was with them too, as he often was. He didn't say much, but he added tone, for he dressed well and smiled in the right places, and we thought his name was elegant. The girls shoved me into the bench first and followed me. I felt secure, hemmed in by friends. I was happy. I beamed at Dwight.

"She doesn't look too worried," Willard said. "Not exactly ready for the funny farm."

"Don't say 'farm,' " I begged. "See—I'm shaking." I held out my hand, which was indeed trembling with excitement, angling it a bit towards Dwight in hopes that he'd take it. He didn't. Well, I could see how it would be awkward for him. Willard Jewell felt my pulse, shook his head, held a paper napkin to his breast in a gesture of final respects.

"All right, boys," Viv said, in her best schoolmarm voice, "let's get on to the problem. Tell us again, Fish."

I told them again. Marcus cracked up. "Once more," he pleaded. I ignored him. I also ignored Jewell, who had turned into a chicken. Though Dwight's eyes were dancing, he managed what seemed to be a sincere gaze of sympathy.

"Chickens," he croaked. "That's too—too—"

I began to laugh myself, and for some minutes all six of us sat and howled and wiped our eyes. I felt better afterwards, and even ordered a Coke.

"Have a hamburger, Fish," Dwight, recovered, said kindly. "I'll pay."

I didn't want a hamburger. I'd have to eat it, for Pete's sake, chew it and swallow it and start it on its unspeakable trip through the gastro-intestinal system. Nothing to be doing in public, in my opinion, let alone in front of the people before whom I most wished to appear super-humanly perfect. But I was touched and I knew enough not to let slip by me something that leaned in the approximate direction of dating. While I hesitated, Dwight had begun to look a little sad. Were boys as uncomfortable as I, perchance?

"Thanks, Dwight," I said, smiling hard. "I'd love it. Well done."

Oh death and hell, would he think I meant "you asked nicely" well done instead of "cook it thoroughly" well done? I felt my face heating up yet again. The girls gave me a look that said, "Isn't Fish cute; Dwight buys her a hamburger and she's blushing." Let them think it. The concept of couple was welcome from any direction.

"All right, I'll confess," Marc said unexpectedly. "I've got some skeletons in my closet too." We all looked at his lanky body and struggled to surpress allusions to bones. Our tact was rewarded by a droll, comprehending grin and a whisper across the booth: "When I'm home I have to babysit my twin nieces. I have to take them downtown in a *stroller*. They drool a lot." His voice fell yet lower. "People think they're mine," he breathed.

"Are they?" I whispered back before I thought.

"No!" he howled, and pounded the table. "You think I'd do it with my own sister? I'm not telling you any more secrets."

"Vice is nice," Jewell sang under his breath.

"It's all right, Marc," Viv said. "You think that's embarrassing—my folks used to send me out collecting when people owed on their bills. They figured nobody would turn down a kid. I used to hate that. Sabra, here," she added, "told us just today that she had to raise a sheep."

Sabra looked as though she would have preferred to do the telling herself. "Well, Viv," she said. "It was only a lamb," she told the boys. "I didn't have it long."

"Nice work, Bo Peep," said Jewell, "but you haven't heard gross yet. My old lady washed my underwear with a pair of red socks and turned it pink. She made me wear it, and I had to carry the flag for my scout troop and my pants fell down right in front of the post office. The kids called me Blush Butt for a year and a half."

Dwight had for some time been visibly struggling to divulge his own secret. We all gave him encouraging glances. "Well," he said, looking down, "don't ever tell anyone else, this is just for the circle, but my folks take in summer guests and they make my brother and sister and me sing for them. It used to be in our pajamas. I guess the other two don't mind, but I could just die from it." There was a sympathetic pause.

"I guess I feel better," I said. "Thanks. But why don't they know? I mean, they do love us, don't they? How can they do this stuff to us?"

"What's love got to do with anything?" Viv snapped. "It's just the way it is."

"Power," leered Marc.

"They forget," sighed Sabra.

"I didn't raise my boy to be a soldier," hummed Jewell.

"But in any case," said Dwight, "we may be able to hold off the great chicken invasion. I can't promise, Fish, but I'll try to stop it."

King Saul must have felt the same struggle of loony hope with common sense when David offered to take on Goliath. I went home happy.

That night I took a notebook into the bathroom with me and wrote by hand while the water ran. No use in pressing matters. I tried to imagine that I was pre-typewriter. Me and Edgar Allan Poe.

> Fearful her thoughts—more fearful yet her dreams, her very imaginings—as Lucilla Shark leaned, nay drooped, across the black, the iron, the cold and enclosing fence whence no denizens issued out, the tenants of the *grave*. And why? Alas her dreams were haunted, her daylight hours made dark, by the image of that final prison so like, so very like, her own joyless and restricted life. Hemmed in on right and left, smothered as under feathers, too torpid and dulled with pain to rouse herself, she could scarce summon the spirit to beat on the padded lid of her existence.

"Padded lid of her existence." I chewed my eraser with glee. The tub was getting full. I'd have to hurry. My pencil flew over the dampening sheets.

But at last a moment arrived—as moments so immemorially do—when light, when joy presented themselves to her fevered brain, for there—there—how shall we speak it, there arrived the love that seems to lay open the grave itself, the grave *of* the self. It was Brownell Flite, Brownell the kind, Brownell the witty, Brownell the longed for, whose incomparable footfall on the horizon, ah *such* a horizon, heralded a return to strength and sanity.

"Ah, Brownell," said Lucilla. "My only love."

Ah, Dwight.

CHAPTER SIX

I didn't do any work on the novel for a few days after
that, partly because I couldn't get my mind off Dwight's
heroic offer or my suspense about whether he could
really save me, and partly because I didn't want to pro-
voke an early attack of chickens before he could do whatever he had in mind. I moved the manuscript from the
scarf drawer to the pajama drawer so I could keep it flat.
I didn't think that even my mother would be poking
around my summer pajamas this late into the year. Once
in a while before I went to sleep I'd sneak the pages out
and reread the adventures of Lucilla Shark. She made
me see bolder possibilities in myself.

That talk in the restaurant had helped a lot. You always hear about teenage girlfriends telling each other
everything they know, but in my experience that's earlier, like about fourth grade, before you begin to worry
that maybe you're the only person in the world who has

certain fears and shynesses. After that you play your cards pretty close to your chest; sometimes you even sit on them, for real safety. (Of course, maybe I was the only person who felt *that* way. There's no end to anxiety.)

One day about a week after that council of war, Dwight caught up with me as I was leaving school.

"Let's have your books," he said, reaching out.

My books. You bet. My hand, my heart, my lasting love. Just ask. Carrying my books, by the way, was no small gesture, because I always took most of them home, preferring to dream and doodle in study hall, when I could get away with it. He made the gesture as though it were a casual thing, but I felt myself stiff with significance as I paced beside him, thinking "Here I am, having my Books Carried Home by the boy I love." This consciousness of occasion tied my tongue to some degree, though now and then I tried to say things designed to stir up his romantic inclinations, if any—"Pretty day" —"Nice clouds"—"Nice bare tree branches." Fruitless ploys, as it turned out. He didn't say much either. Was this love, the great chicken rout, or both?

"You want to come in a while?" I ventured as we crunched up the driveway.

"I guess I've got time," he said.

My mother was pleased to see us. She got out the cookie jar and a big bottle of Coke, and when Dwight said, "You'll join us, won't you, Mrs. Fisher?" she did.

I could tell she liked him. This was the first time he'd actually been in our house, but she acted natural. Perhaps she even felt natural; she wasn't in love with him. I didn't mind her staying there. It made me less tense, and besides, what can happen at a kitchen table even if the family's in the other room? A little finger touching at best, and we hadn't progressed even to that stage of declaration. For me it was exciting enough seeing Dwight materialized in places where I'd only dreamed about him.

My mother, by asking questions that I couldn't and adults quite casually could, found out the following things:

> Dwight's mother had been a teacher. (Mine too!)
> He had skipped a grade in school. (Me too!)
> He was the eldest child in his family. (Me too!)

How could anybody have a clearer mandate from the great dating service in the sky? Okay, I know none of that looks like anything (He has two eyes and a nose. Me too!), but a fact attached to Dwight was a fact glorified. I was very far gone. I tried without staring to take in every detail of him as he sat there, and to imagine the secret workings of his mysterious internal engines. To think that a billion random chances had harmonized to make this prodigy! And he breathed, he talked, he drank Coke— what a miracle! I could have fallen down on the kitchen floor and worshiped him. Hard to be subtle about that, though. Hard to just slip off your chair and get in a quick genuflection, a fast forehead touch to the linoleum, a little lick at the soles of his white bucks, while pretending to tie your shoe. I sipped my Coke and basked instead.

Meanwhile, we all, for our different reasons, had an ear towards the door, waiting for my father. Whenever the door knob rattled we jumped. The first time it was Herbie, who looked a little shy at the sight of Dwight but took three cookies on his way to the TV.

The next time it was Grannie Hatch, from next door. I held my breath. She was really quite, quite mad, but my mother always let her wander in, often straight through the house and out the front door. "I'll be old and crazy some day and won't want people locking me out," my mother would say. The reason I held my breath (aside from Grannie Hatch's careless stance about personal hygiene) was that she always did one of two things—spoke in rhyme, or told the same joke. I wasn't sure which one Dwight would take better.

"Is there anything going on tonight?" she asked. It was the joke, then.

"Not that I know of, Mrs. Hatch," said my dutiful mother, playing straight man.

"Over our heads at nine o'clock!" Grannie Hatch cackled, and was gone.

There was a silence. "Well, it's certainly over *my* head," said Dwight at last. "What was that about? Or is it some kind of secret?"

"Not a secret," I said, laughing. "Just a sort of code because she's told the same joke so often. 'Over our heads at nine o'clock' is code for the real punchline, which is 'Oh yes there is, our nightgowns.' Nightgowns going on— get it?"

Amazing. I didn't mind mentioning nightgowns to Dwight, not at all. Though of course any nightgown the old lady pulled over her demented head would be pretty modest. But with Dwight there, a bed was a piece of furniture and no more. Not that lying down beside Dwight wouldn't be a fantastic thing to do. Or standing up. Or just sitting there.

"You have interesting neighbors," he said. "But seriously, I've seen her out hitchhiking. Doesn't anybody take care of her?" You could see my mother thinking that he was one considerate guy, which of course I knew already. He was always the one of us who was worried about people's feelings. He'd probably been that way since he could talk. I briefly imagined him as a short, courteous, bespectacled child, and cut off the vision when it began to turn into a flock of short, courteous, bookish children that Dwight and I might produce together.

Grannie Hatch's bizarre routine was good for conversation, though. We all three traded stories of eccentrics and madmen and snorted into our sodas. Mom and I had a fine collection of our own, and Dwight, who came from the coast, added some old skippers who *would* use nautical terms in all circumstances— "I've got a pain on my starboard side, Doctor"—and ludicrous tourists. Still we listened for my father, or at any rate Dwight and I did. If he didn't come soon, Dwight would have to get back to the dorm for supper.

After a while Dwight and I moved into the living room and Mom began to make rolls. I itched around the room, turning the television on and off, bringing Dwight things to look at, admiring his new watch and praying that its hands would move slowly. But my father did come at last and sat down in his usual chair, smiling warmly at my guest. I should say that although my father could embarrass me with kinky rules and projects, he never in any fashion misbehaved with any of my friends. With them he was generous, welcoming, deferential. I began to feel a creeping hope that Dwight (who by now was obviously here for the chicken project) might really do it.

"Mr. Fisher," Dwight said respectfully after Dad was settled into his chair, "your daughter tells me that she might be raising chickens." I was astonished—what a bold, frontal attack! Was he really going to take Dad on? Maybe he *did* love me.

"We have," said my father, "been thinking about a few Plymouth Rocks."

"Plymouth Rocks are pretty nice hens, I guess," Dwight said politely. (Was he faking it? Did he really know anything about Plymouth Rocks?) "Makes you

think of the Puritans and all that.'' (Nope, he didn't.)
''My father has a few Rhode Island Reds,'' he went on
somewhat wildly. ''Makes you think of the McCarthy
hearings.''

My father laughed. ''I don't think your hens can be
held against you.'' Dwight was warming him up. Wow.

''I guess it's my grandmother who should have the
Puritan chickens,'' he went on. ''Talk about your Puritan work ethic. She thinks work fixes everything that can
go wrong with a person—hangnails, measles, night-
mares.''

Very brave, Dwight, very bold. My father, who believed precisely those things himself, was smiling a little
more guardedly. Dwight got a grip on his shield and
lance and rode forth yet again to save me. He looked as
innocent and wide-eyed as Beaver Cleaver.

''Did I ever tell you,'' he said, turning to me, ''about
the time my grandmother made me raise cabbages?''

''Cabbages?'' I echoed, as though we'd rehearsed.

''She thought that if I worked hard raising cabbages
and then sold them and kept the money, why then I'd
like to work and have pleasant associations with it.''

''Not,'' he added, ''that I ever really minded working.
I mean, at something that made sense.''

''Didn't the cabbages make sense?'' I helped.

''Not exactly,'' he said, ''because everyone in town
had cabbages already. You might say that I learned about
supply and demand, though. See, here I had raised these

five hundred cabbages or so, and I could only sell about a dozen, and I think the neighbors just took those to be nice.''

"What did you do with five hundred cabbages?" I couldn't help asking, even though it might be a digression.

"We stored them in the cellar in case there was a major cabbage shortage later. After they rotted, we shoveled them out for three days. What a mess!''

"Of course," he added, "Fish probably wouldn't have such a bad problem with eggs, I'm sure she wouldn't, even though I guess quite a few people around here keep chickens themselves. And five hundred eggs don't take up as much room as five hundred, well maybe four hundred and eighty-eight cabbages, and you could keep them in the refrigerator—"

"But I'll tell one thing," he announced, getting back on track with a triumphant note, "I really didn't like to work nearly as well as I had before, when I got through with those cabbages. I mean, what had it all been for? I know my grandmother meant well and all, but I had to raise those cabbages just to humor her, and I was kind of bitter about it. I don't think, do you, Mr. Fisher, that there's much point in work that there isn't any use for? Not that there wouldn't be a use for those eggs, I don't mean.''

"Quite a story," my father admitted. "I'll have to give this matter some thought. You may have a point about market.''

Holy cow! He'd really done it! David had brought down Goliath with a grin and a slingshot. I was dizzy with admiration, and I made myself one promise right then. If I ever got married, it would be to somebody who made me feel as protected as Dwight did. That, or I wouldn't do it at all.

We sailed through the kitchen to the back door on a wave of good feeling. When we were out of earshot I tried to speak, but it was hard to get words through my manic grin.

"Dwight," I said. "Dwight."

I reached out a tentative hand, to do what, I couldn't have said, but Dwight took it and squeezed it, and I saw that it was for that.

"It wasn't anything," he said, but he looked pleased. "I almost lost it there with the Rhode Island Reds," he said.

We began to laugh together. He dropped my hand and only our voices touched. Then he zipped up his jacket and was off down the driveway, my knight, in danger of a reprimand for lateness. But I thought he could stand up to that too.

Before I could do justice to this chapter, I'd have to re-read *The Idylls of the King*.

CHAPTER SEVEN

Every time I talk about one thing—chickens, say, or Dwight—I'm neglecting all the other things that were still happening at the same time. The daily satisfactions and pride of being with Sabra and Viv, for instance. The slimy insinuations about the preferences of cowboys. But one day in November, not too long before Thanksgiving, these heretofore parallel lines met, even collided.

It was a gray day with an edge to it, but for gloom and edginess it had nothing on me. I was sensitive as an unshelled turtle. Hormones, I guess. If people looked at me when they should have looked away, or looked away from me when they should have looked at me, I brimmed with tears and rage. Once, before afternoon classes even began, I had to shut myself in a toilet stall and flush the toilet while I wiped my eyes on the sleeve of my blouse. Not even I knew what had set that off.

Certainly it was nothing that Sabra and Viv had done, for they were being especially sweet to me, and a good thing too. For instance, they looked at my essay for English and told me I could really write. I felt good for a while then. The essay was a description of an accident I'd seen the summer before, with a whole lot of people flocking out in the night to look at it. I called it "Accidents Is Awful Things to Happen," after my favorite line of overheard conversation. To me it meant both "they're awful things when they happen" and "they sure do have a propensity for happening." It would have been a bad day for anybody to tease me about the grammar in the title. Viv and Sabra didn't. They knew sophistication when they saw it.

"I'll write about us all some day," I said. I had my secrets.

"We believe you," they told me, and I could see that they did. I was proud to be believed by friends so elegant, with the pleats of their skirts like razors and their socks all neatly cuffed. I loved them.

On the down side, two sophomores dared to ask me what cowboys liked, and when I went to chemistry I saw that someone had scrawled "Get it up cowboys" on the stairwell wall. Lucilla Shark would have had something to say about that.

I was supposed to go to Viv and Sabra's room after school to plot some innovations for graduation; we had found that advance planning meant power. I knew I'd be better off to go home, but they seemed safe company and I'd grown calmer in the course of the afternoon. On the way out we stopped in the home-ec room to pick up some forks for a dorm party. People drifted in and out there at the end of the day, just in case someone had made extra cookies, and we let ourselves be swept into the sociability. I was hoping that Dwight would come by. He sometimes did.

I perched on the edge of a table, keeping an eye on the door and playing with the pleats of my skirt while Viv and Sabra bustled about at the other end of the room. Mine was a reversible skirt, both new and fairly expensive, and I liked it. The side I usually turned out was gray, but its neutral pleats opened to show slashes of the reverse side's red plaid. I smoothed the pleats together to cover the red, let them loose to flash their color. In my absentminded vanity, I must have looked like a peacock playing with its tail. I attribute a little of what happened to that factor. And I was making myself feel aloof on purpose, sitting higher than other people, getting ready to run for the door if I felt emotional.

There was half a pitcher of Kool-Aid on the table (somebody tackling the simpler culinary problems of real life), and I sipped a bit out of a paper cup and told myself that pretty soon I'd be out of there and into the increasingly soothing sequence of Viv and Sabra's room, my house, my room.

Two boys came and sat by the Kool-Aid pitcher. Two boys with Elvis Presley hair and knowing smirks. Two scumbags, in fact. Leroy Richardson and George Paston. They were as far from being Dwight as people of the same age and sex could get. I said hello, at least I probably did, but they were ostensibly talking to each other and I tuned them out with all my might.

"Did you hear about the crab that broke its legs and had to walk around on crotches?"

Yuk, yuk. Snarf, snarf.

"It was Christmas eve and everyone was feeling Mary."

Snort, snort. Titter, titter.

I sipped the last of my Kool-Aid and went on sipping at air, keeping busy, hiding my hot face in my cup.

"Long, wicked long, guess who's wicked long?"

"Oh ho, Richardson!"

"Oh you George, wicked long!"

They'd be getting to cowboys next, I supposed. Maybe I could leave first. And then I heard what I suddenly knew to be Dwight's steps in the corridor and shyly looked away from the door, pleased to pieces that I knew his steps from everyone else's. There's love for you. I'd blessedly lost track of the scumbag conversation, but now through my haze I saw Leroy's face before mine, an angry face, a face that hadn't liked being ignored. He sounded vicious as he leaned forward and hissed, "Did you hear me?"

I shook my head.

"I said, 'Your friends Viv and Sabra are cowboying around Augusta every weekend.' What do you think of that?"

I'd read enough to recognize a thrown gauntlet. Time
slowed and I saw everyone clearly while I revolved what
to do—Dwight in the doorway, Sabra and Viv outraged
beside the refrigerator, Leroy's slavering lips that had
just uttered such blasphemy. What I did wasn't impulsive
at all, as everyone assumed later. It was a clear, Lucilla
Shark decision to stop sitting on the sidelines of the action and take a stand, join in. I picked up the pitcher of
Kool-Aid and emptied it over his face, giving his greasy
head a little whack with the empty pitcher for punctua-
tion, not hard enough to crack his skull and let the bugs
out, but enough to show I wasn't kidding.

I can see now several reasons why I did it. It was one
cowboy remark too many. It was an attack on my adored
friends. It was said out of meanness. But more than these
things, I couldn't bear the suggestion that my friends,
my Viv and Sabra, were doing, *doing*, things that I
couldn't even stand to talk about. That they should be
on the other side, with scumbags and insinuators, was
not a tolerable thought.

The sensation of rage caught up with me only after
the world began to move again, and then it made my
knees shake. I slid from the table and held onto a chair
to steady myself as I looked around at the amazing scene
I'd brought about. Leroy's head was bleeding in dra-
matic quantities, and although I remembered that head
wounds do that and it doesn't mean that the bleeder is
killed, I was a little taken aback as it sheeted over his

forehead with the Kool-Aid. The Kool-Aid was red, too, but not the same shade or density as his blood. It seemed possible that I was going to be in trouble. Leroy looked dazed. Peering through the torrent from his forehead, he was chasing an ice cube down the front of his shirt. He was bound to holler soon. Had I thrown myself outside decent society forever?

Then Sabra and Viv were beside me. Sabra squeezed my hand. "Thanks, Fish," she whispered. To hell with decent society, then.

Viv had her fists on her hips, considering the medical problem. "Well, my lord, Fish, I appreciate it too," she said, "but don't you think you went a little too far? Somebody get some dish towels. It serves you right, Leroy."

Her tart tones got us all moving. Dwight beat me to the dish towel drawer, for I was still a little shaky. I hardly dared look at him. Would he think I was the she-devil of the western world? Would he ever like me again? I cared about that, despite the lunatic high I still felt from bashing Leroy. (Death to Cowboys. Do you love me, then?) But Dwight had thrown his arm across my shoulders for a quick, reassuring hug.

"You're quite a fighter," he grinned. "Whap. Pow. Glad I got here in time to see it." What a relief.

Leroy kept his mouth shut while we—mostly Viv—mopped him none too gently off. We were almost done when the principal came in. The intensity of his "All right, what's happened here?" made me see that my trouble might be major. I was mostly so bookish and well behaved that adults didn't shoot that tone in my direction. Now he was making serious principal noises.

Viv's quick wits were up to it. "Fish dropped the pitcher and it hit Leroy," she said. "I don't think any real damage was done, Mr. Judson."

"The pitcher isn't broken!" I said, and burst into lucky, convincing tears. They'd probably be taken for remorse, not just fear and a hard day.

Leroy kept his mouth shut. Maybe not a total scumbag.

"Just slipped out of her hands, sir," Sabra added. "I saw it."

"Me too," Dwight said. "What a splash! Poor old Leroy."

Leroy's buddy George was silent for once. Probably he enjoyed the sight of anyone's blood.

"Well," said Mr. Judson, who could tell something was wrong but knew when to quit, "you haven't any business fooling around in here after school anyway. You see what happens. Clean up and get out of here."

"And you," he said to Leroy, "come along and have the nurse take a look. Don't drip on the floor. It's my experience that you have a pretty hard head." Leroy tried a wan grin. He and his friend left.

The rest of us gazed at each other with relief.

"Quit blubbering, Fish," said Viv. "Nothing to worry about now; he won't tell. Give me those dish towels, Dwight, and I'll put them to soak in the sink, and then let's get out of here.''

Sabra was straightening chairs and putting the shades right. "You were loyal, Fish," she said.

"I admit it," said Viv. "Not everyone would have tried to kill the garbage mouth. What a mess."

"Fish is pretty special," said Dwight.

"She's that, all right," said Viv a little grimly. But I knew she was pleased, all the same. I began to dry my eyes on my shoulder. Gosh, I was tired.

We skipped the planning session. It was late. The others needed restaurant coffee. I needed solitude. I slipped through the downstairs and up to my room, where I flopped on the bed. I was too tired to set up the typewriter, but that didn't mean I couldn't plan.

"It was a far, far better thing she did," I whispered to the ceiling, "than she had ever done before." Me and Charles Dickens.

CHAPTER EIGHT

I waited all evening for the ringing of the phone, for Mr. Judson breaking it to my parents—"Your daughter, in the home-ec room, with the Kool-Aid pitcher," a horrible real-life game of Clue. But the phone never rang, and nobody made any bread-and-water jokes at breakfast.

I was halfway afraid to go to school that morning, but also halfway eager, as if I'd put down a book at a suspenseful point and wanted to see what would happen next. As I suspected, everyone at school knew about Leroy. November is a dull month. Where I walked, heads turned and smart alecks ducked. Cowboys? What cowboys? Nobody in my hearing dared to allude to anything west of the Mississippi or south of the waist. Viv and Sabra stuck pretty close, and so did Dwight. I'd never felt so much a celebrity. The man from *Time* might come any day now. Good thing my tennis racket was ready.

I felt taller, and although I was deep in guilty-teenager embarrassment, I also felt more adult. I had stepped over into a world where I took action, instead of just doing what people expected. Previously I'd now and then screwed up, or argued about something I perceived as a principle, nose to nose with a teacher, but nobody had bled. Nobody had had to lie for me or soak dish towels in cold water.

The first class was Advanced Math, and we had a test, so that was fairly safe. Viv and Dwight were in that class, and Dwight changed his seat to sit behind me, like a shield. I could relax, knowing that he was between me and the rest of the people. On the way out of class a couple of guys made a show of climbing over each other to get out of my way, but Dwight shot them a look and took my elbow.

His next class was downstairs, but he walked with Viv and me to my history class, where Sabra was waiting. I felt a diminishing of safety when Dwight left. Though Viv and Sabra were tough and loyal and there were two of them, he had a better grip on the boys. Girls were no problem; one or two of them said, "Good for you!" or "Give it to him, Fish!" but most of them kept still. I was almost to my seat when a voice from the back cracked, "And now Miss Fisher will tell us about the Pubic—er, the Punic Wars." It was Willard Jewell, of

course, but he wasn't mean, just irrepressible, so that
was okay, sort of. I cast him a half smile before I sat
down. I opened my book and read it with a fervor that
shut out the classroom. I had no idea what it said—can
an ostrich report on the sand around its head?—but I'd
already studied it anyway. I was aware of Sabra and
Viv sitting very straight, looking ready for a fight. The
Missouri Compromise passed by my ears. Compromise?
Never!

Third period was study hall. That would be tough, for
there we sat in assigned seats. I liked the teacher who
supervised, but I didn't put much faith in his protection.
He was strange—that was what I liked—a man perhaps
in his early sixties, with a wild eye and an unpredictable
tongue. He was one of those people who show up sometimes in a teenager's life bearing hints of inconceivable
freedom in the adult world, the possibility of never doing
the expected and thriving anyway. Once I heard him, in
the middle of a blizzard, shouting at the janitor through
the snow, "Flog your wife! Flog your wife! She *said* it
was going to snow!" Half way through the period he
stopped by my seat and grinned a grin of complicity,
without saying a word. Did he see in me a fledgling
weirdo, as I saw in him possibilities of a later self? Nobody teased me. I got a little work done.

Fourth period was English. Sabra was in my section,
and when I came out of study hall she was loitering near
the door in a coincidental-looking way and walked with

me. From the other end of the corridor Dwight saw her, smiled, and nodded. English was always good. My territory. I'd already spot-read through the anthology, could flip the pages and find friends. "Go down to Kew in lilac-time (it isn't far from London!)/ And you shall wander hand in hand with love in summer's wonderland . . . ." You bet. Or now, even, without the lilacs. If you wandered hand in hand with love in November, it would seem like summer.

Of course in English there were a few jokes—*The Pitcher of Dorian Gray*, "The Charge of the Kool-Aid Brigade," and so on. Not brilliant wit, but not too scary either. The teacher was in her first year out of college, but she had fairly good control of the class, and since we'd first made her laugh, broken her in, she'd been okay. We were doing "The Rime of the Ancient Mariner," and I must confess that the slimy things crawling on the sea did make me think a little of Leroy. Coleridge seemed to suggest that I wasn't allowed to hate him, but indeed I halfway liked him since I'd taken out my frustration on him and he hadn't made a fuss. I still didn't like the things he had to say, though. I was the opposite of the Mariner, compelled, not to open my mouth, but to close my ears.

Towards the end of noon break, when people were drifting back to home room and I was already hiding out at my desk, I looked up to find Dwight beside me. As nobody had yet taken the seat ahead of me, he sat in it sideways and turned to face me.

"You doing okay?" he asked.

"I guess so," I said. "Everybody's being real nice. You too."

He shrugged it away. "Your parents know?"

"I sure hope not."

"I don't think anybody'd tell them, do you?"

"Not unless Judson does, and I guess he would have by now if he were going to."

"I don't think even Judson would want to hurt *you*, Fish."

While I took in the implications of that kind remark, Dwight was hunting for something in his shirt pocket. Having found it, he held it out to me in the palm of his hand. It was a little round pin about half an inch across, rimmed with decorative knobs.

"I found this in the restaurant," he said, looking embarrassed. "You can have it."

Me? Me? My heart bumped against my white blouse. I grinned like a fool, I think. Me, of all the people he could have given it to. He made it sound like a Cracker Jack prize, and I didn't care if it was—it felt like the Kohinoor diamond. I took it, hoping that the sudden sweat on my palm wouldn't wash it away, and with some difficulty fastened it through the collar of my blouse.

"Thanks," I said. "It's neat." Oh, the inadequacy of words!

That night I laid it in my pink-lined jewelry box, where the wind-up ballerina could guard it. It was too holy to wear. I looked at it a long time before I put it away. Not 14 karat, but no Cracker Jack prize. Had he really found it? Could he possibly have got it on purpose? Never mind, it had sat in a pocket over his heart and he'd chosen me to give it to. One of life's more encouraging moments.

I felt that something had been said (Are we engaged, Ma?), but I didn't know what. That led me to further thoughts about the difference between life and art. Or at least off and on it did. I thought about life and art, and then I thought about Dwight. I thought about life and art and what it would be like to be a madly successful author. And I thought about life and art and my new blue skirt's possible erotic effect on Dwight. And I thought about life and art and some Band-Aids I'd seen in colors and shapes, and whether I'd dare to stick a red heart on Dwight's hand. But in spite of all the pleasant detours, I did come to some conclusions. My earlier idea that life was fuzzy and undramatic compared to art was only part of the truth.

There were some things, like the giving and receiving of a little round gold pin, that nobody—not I, Lawrence, Poe, Dickens, whoever—could catch the glory behind. Art couldn't in fact do those things as *well* as life. I don't know what those medieval scholars decided about how many angels could dance on the head of a pin, but there were five or six dozen on the pin that Dwight gave me. Probably they were still hoofing it up in the box with the ballerina. What can you say about stuff like that? Maybe a poet could do it, but I wasn't a poet, and none of the rhymes for "pin" were very romantic, anyway.

I searched the stories I knew for love scenes where the participants couldn't quite tell what had happened, though they knew that something had. About all I could think of was Anne of Green Gables' daughter Rilla wondering whether she was engaged when a boy told her not to kiss anyone else. Or maybe the lovely weaver in *Precious Bane* telling Prue Sarn, "It must be toerts, not frommert." I could see why writers didn't get into it much. Like me, they preferred Heathcliffe/Catherine explicitness. I could make the pin something bigger, but I couldn't make it anything better.

After supper I went to my room and intensified my mood by playing records (a teenage frailty that not even my father would find suspicious): *Love Is a Golden Ring*, *Cherry Pink and Apple-Blossom White*, *You Don't Know Me*—all my sentimental stuff. Then I took my pencil and tried, but the result was only different from life, not more magical.

> "I found this in Cambridge," he said, "in the gift shop of the Harvard Museum, where I'd gone to see the glass flowers."
>
> As the apple blossoms drifted down around them she took it in her hands, a string of golden amber beads and enameled flowers.

"It's the most beautiful thing I ever saw," she breathed.

"That's why I thought of you," he said. "Let me fasten it around your throat myself."

Her heart dancing a mazurka against her white silk dress, she bowed her head in unaccustomed submission. His hands burned into her skin. "He is a part of me," she thought.

"It's a circle now," he said. "Circles mean perfection, and they never end, like our love. Never in this world or the next. We'll haunt each other."

"I hope so," Lucilla said.

CHAPTER NINE

When Christmas vacation came, it was a wrench to be separated from all the people who mattered most to me right then, but the emotional rest was not altogether unwelcome. Of course, there are limits to how much rest a person wants. With the school shut, my home town was a bleak and empty place. Public Christmas decorations consisted of one string of colored lights from the post office to the phone pole across the street. It swung and lashed in the snow-laden wind, and now and then a bulb broke. One year the town had a small, lighted tree on the roof of the post office porch, but it blew down so often that they never tried it again. Funny, I hadn't noticed the wind and snow and bleakness so much when the other kids were around.

As you might imagine, the post office was the focus not only of town decorations but also of my hopes and longings. The mail came twice a day, around eight in the morning and four in the afternoon. That meant that my folks had already brought home the earlier lot, along with the newspaper, when I got up, and my first act was to scan the kitchen table for envelopes addressed to me. I usually volunteered to go for the afternoon mail, an experience so intense that sometimes I still dream I'm standing there, peering into our box. Usually so little mail came in the afternoon that my mother said it wasn't worth crossing the street for, but she wasn't seventeen (which I was now, almost). I watched for Christmas cards from my special friends the way I used to watch for ones with glitter when I was little. Every year I saved the most emotionally crucial half dozen in an envelope in my bottom bureau drawer.

This year I got one from Dwight, a new experience despite our several years of friendship. Holly, candles— your generic Christmas card, except that inside there was his dear, distinctive signature, "Dwight Brown." Not "Love, Dwight," but then, I'd sent him a card and I hadn't signed it "Love, Fish" either. I spent some time in fruitless speculation about whether he'd had my card before he sent his, whether he was just responding or would have sent one anyway. There was no way to know. Never mind, I had it.

Christmas was one time I didn't really itch to leave home, though still the vision persisted of shapelier trees than ours, city lights, silver bells, and Dickensian geese and plum puddings. But we were all of us pursuing a halting version of the same vision, I suppose, and we had our traditions.

A week or two before Christmas we'd put up our tree, and local custom decreed its coming down on the 26th; that usually happened before I was out of bed, and I'd wake up to find Christmas gone. It was a clean end. One year the Judsons actually got a tree shaped like the ones on the cards and I was astounded; I guess I'd thought they were some kind of trick photography. Ours were often oddly shaped—we suspected Dad of cutting down the first tree he came to—and once, but once only, we had a tree larger at the top than the bottom, very disorienting. But they smelled good, and the decorations were all old friends—the pink ball painted with water lilies that had been on my mother's first tree, the fuzzy candy cane given to me one surprising day by the town hooker, Santa's head made out of an egg by an artistic family friend, the plain balls and the striped ones, the bubble lights (we all liked the purple one best), the mangy strings of tinsel. Our icicles went on in clumps, for we usually forgot to buy them, had to drive to the next town when we remembered, and at last got bored and threw them. Mom and Herbie and I trimmed the tree. Dad sat in his chair and watched. He'd done his bit.

Over the years Herbie and I had reached a truce with our incompatible Christmas personalities. When I was little I was up every half hour all night, wanting to know if Santa had come. Herbie wanted to put on his shoes and have his oatmeal before he looked in his stocking. He must have been easier, but his was a minority attitude. One year when he was very young he'd stopped in the middle of his presents and said he guessed he'd save the rest. "You open!" we all snarled at him. He sighed and went on.

I had some good memories of loving gestures. Once my father took his boot and made a big sooty Santa Claus footprint on the hearth. Once during the war, before Herbie was born, when sugar was rationed and you couldn't buy candy canes, my mother and grandmother had made them for me, or tried to; I can still see that candy cane, pale pink and white, wilting over the side of the stocking.

We still hung stockings, even though I was old for it—red skating socks. They lent a pleasant taste of festivity while Dad went to get my grandparents. When they came, we had our presents. It was a time in my life when I was getting clothes, jewelry, coveted books, occasionally an animal for my bed, and I was so attuned to all those things that I could almost taste them. Herbie and I each had a card table that we could put our things on, a ploy devised when we were younger, I guess, to keep them off the floor.

Under the tree I had silverware-shaped boxes from Viv and Sabra, gift-wrapped in the distinctive style of the best jewelry shop in fifty miles. Their thick polished paper and dense little pre-fab bows always made Christmas more glamorous. My freshman year I'd had a box from there with a really good bracelet, a gold chain with half a dozen semiprecious polished stones hanging from it: lapis lazuli, goldstone, malachite, and so on. A pretty thing, and I had secretly studied it and chosen a stone for each of the people I loved that year, so that I carried them with me on my wrist and could count them. I would have made a good Victorian, all covered with hair brooches.

I had excellent presents this year, a dark gray crew-neck sweater, a Ouija board, two hard-cover volumes of Edna St. Vincent Millay's poems. My grandmother had bought me the most alluring thing I'd ever had to sleep in, yellow nylon baby-doll pajamas, the short top and panties ruffly and transparent and shiny, the height of frivolous fashion, and the kind of thing my mother and even the sales clerks had said I could have when I got married. Why should she wait, my grandmother said. Ha ha, Mom. There were other things, a *Roget's Thesaurus*, more clothes, a fun bracelet with a strip of mink wound through the links. I remember being happy.

Being happy at home, I should add, didn't have any serious effect on my long-term longing to be out of there. The two feelings just existed side by side in my head. I don't think it was entirely clear to me that I'd have to leave one happiness to have the other. I couldn't imagine me not at home, though I could readily imagine me bopping down the streets of Manhattan, two simultaneous lives.

After Christmas I tried to make some progress on my novel. This was beginning to be difficult because of the cold. Our upstairs wasn't heated. Most local second stories weren't, partly at least because the homeowners had grown up with clammy bedrooms and preferred them. There was one furnace vent in the hall, a sensuous pleasure to stand over on the way back from the bathroom, letting the hot air blow up inside one's flannel nightgown. Sometimes, if we were feeling frail, we took hot water bottles to bed, touching our feet to the boiling-hot rubber and snatching them off again, but chilly, slightly damp-feeling sheets were the norm. If I wanted privacy with a friend, we just left our jackets on and went up and sat on the bed and talked.

But authors who compose in freezing garrets do not occupy garrets over their mothers' houses, for mothers seem to worry about people who want to sit in the cold and the damp by themselves. "If you're working on something, bring it on down," she'd advise. Sensible advice, but not possible. I found out I could stay up there about half an hour at a time before she began to worry about my health. Obviously night health and day health had different rules.

So I alternated scenes of passion with thank-you notes, fine for writing at the kitchen table, and I read and sampled and got stylistic ideas. Sabra and Viv were only about forty miles away, but none of us had our own cars and there was no public transport. I had two letters from

Sabra, written in brown ink in reply to my green ink. Viv was no letter writer. I'd get about one note a summer in her square, lucid writing. I could hear her voice in my mind—"Well, my lord, Fish, if I had anything I needed to say I could call you, couldn't I?"

I could have been two hundred, five hundred miles away from them, once the school closed and my world shut down. When I looked out at the girls' dorm, its windows were black. Dwight was on hold. I was saving my gray sweater for school, my yellow pajamas for summer. The Millay I read and fairly wallowed in, longing for the Greenwich Village of my dreams, but not with the sharp-edged restlessness of my summers.

Of course the love poems were potent—"Women have loved before as I love now"—though an awful lot of them seemed to involve going to bed with people, even lots of people. I picked and chose. But in any case, Millay's poems about sex weren't gross. She kept talking about people's *arms*. I could relate to arms. "When treacherous queens, with death upon the tread,/ Heedless and wilful, took their knights to bed" was a far cry from "Get it up cowboys."

The poems about nature and longing and death made sense to me. Nature always took me out of myself, and I knew about longing for sure. As for death, didn't I worry about it every time my friends went home on a stormy day? But for me the best poems were the New York ones, the poems about a free and bohemian life.

"We were very tired, we were very merry—/ We had gone back and forth all night on the ferry." Can you grasp it? Nobody was making those people pack it in for the night. Nobody was asking them *why* for goodness' sake they wanted to go back and forth all night on the ferry, or whether they needed their sweaters, or how they thought they were going to stay awake the next day. They just rode and giggled all night until the sun came up, and there they were, those friends, still together. I could taste freedom, reading it. I must have read that poem about fifty times. One snowy night the Staten Island Ferry got mixed up in my dreams with Dwight's father's lobstering boat, and Dwight and I rode back and forth in the canals of Venice, holding hands. I think he was going to kiss me just as I woke up.

That vacation was a time of peace and pleasantness, watching "The Honeymooners" and "I Love Lucy," playing cribbage at the kitchen table with my father, tormenting Herbie, sleeping late in my body-warmed sheets and waking to the smell of my mother's molasses cookies. But I must admit that when, on the night before classes began, the dorm windows began to light up, when I could see Viv and Sabra's silhouettes behind their drawn shades, back safe and sound, I was one happy person. I couldn't know about Dwight yet, of course, but it seemed reasonable to assume that he too was back in one piece. Every time a window lighted up, a little candle inside me lighted with joy, and when I went to sleep in full blaze it felt like Christmas Eve all over again.

CHAPTER TEN

In all these weeks I'd been in love with Dwight, we hadn't touched each other much. A few quick, comradely hugs, a little leaning together, a hand-squeeze or two—that was it. While there was no certainty that Dwight loved me, he did seem fond of me; and then, I hadn't told him how I felt either, had I? Up to a point I appreciated this restraint and admired it, but, as I said of restfulness over vacation, there's a limit to how much non-activity a person wants. The fact is, I was beginning to feel painfully unkissed, though I was far from being an across-the-board kissing enthusiast.

You can talk about young love all you want, but if you're honest you'll admit that high school is not peak time for skilled kissing. And what teenage Casanovas lack in finesse they try to make up in vigor. I had been walked home by a number of boys and had some basis for generalization. Oh, those wrestlings at the back door, me holding my breath and shutting my eyes until the kiss was over and whoever-it-was had reeled his endless, wet tongue back into his own mouth. And yet those sticky, salivary sessions on the doorstep seemed an unavoidable part of life, one of the things a girl had to accept gracefully, like menstrual cramps and panty girdles; the fifties were a big time for female acceptance.

"You've got to climb right back on the horse after you've been thrown," I'd tell myself as I walked up the drive with somebody else, knowing what would probably happen and remembering the last time. I meant to be a good sport. A year or two earlier I hadn't even been able to wait to get in the house before I wiped off my tongue. As soon as the boy was gone down the driveway I'd duck around the corner and try to spit away the sensation of being gagged with a wet dishcloth, hoping all the same that somebody or other would walk me home next time. Wet dishcloth doesn't quite capture the sensation, it's not slippery enough, but it's symbolically appropriate, because girls who took to these things too smoothly were likely to find themselves chained to a dishpan for the next fifty years.

That was another thing I had some misgivings about: marriage. It seemed to be full of things I didn't like to do. Domestic things, I mean.

"I hate ironing," I'd say.

"Get used to it. You'll have to iron day and night when you're married." That's my mother, or a neighbor, or any woman a generation or two older than I.

"Then I don't want to get married," I'd say.

"Why of course you want to get married!" the woman would say, shocked. "You'll love it!"

Anyway, to get back to kissing, I worked hard at mind control and after a while I didn't have to spit before I went in the house. I could just hold my breath and go straight for my toothbrush. Now that I was a senior, I could quite often say hello to my parents on the way to the bathroom.

Bearing all this in mind, can you imagine how much I loved Dwight if kissing even entered my imagination as a desirable thing to do? I'd find myself sneaking looks at his lips during math, wondering what it would be like, wanting the contact.

Then, one night early in the new year, I went to a basketball game. I don't know now whom we played against, and I hardly knew then, for Viv and Sabra had not gone home for the weekend and the three of us sat on the bleachers behind the boys, and while the rest of the world studied lay-ups and foul shots, I studied the back of Dwight. The darkness of his hair, how it lay, the set of his neck on his shoulders, the tilt of his ears. I'd never had a chance like this before. We all bantered and joked between moments of athletic suspense, and once Dwight leaned back and I had the sweet weight of him against my knees. I put my hands on his shoulders briefly.

"You have some nice bumps on the back of your head, Dwight," I said.

"Don't look at my head!" he said, blushing.

"Don't you know about phrenology?" I asked craftily.

Practical Viv began to sputter at my foolishness, but Sabra gave her a poke and she caught on. Sabra could always spot a line.

In fact, I knew very little about phrenology myself. "Well," I said, "everyone has bumps on his head, and people used to think you could tell personality stuff from it, like the memory section sticks up a lot or a little, or you're hot-tempered, or sneaky."

"*I'm* sneaky," Dwight said dreamily, watching the game.

"Doesn't look to me like there's any sneakiness bump," I said, seizing the excuse I'd been waiting for and running my finger down the back of his head.

"I'm so sneaky I hide the bump," he joked, but I was too shaken by touching his hair to banter back. I was used to girls' hair, I guess, to my own hair, to the far ends of it that I put curlers on. Dwight's was so close to his head, felt so warm and lived-in, that it seemed to have its own pulse.

"What's that bump on *your* head, Jewell?" said Sabra, pointing to it.

"Why that's my mathematical bump," said Willard. "Coach bashed me there with an algebra book in study hall."

We all milled around a bit after the game was over, and I lost sight of Dwight. I didn't want to leave alone

if there was any chance of his walking me home, so I
tied and retied my shoes, wound and rewound my scarf,
blew my nose—in short, delayed. Ah, he was talking to
one of the players. Would he never stop?

But at last my diversionary tactics worked and he was
at my elbow. "I had to talk to Spence," he said. "He
was feeling bad about that foul shot. I'm glad you
waited. I'll walk you home."

See that? He knew what I was doing and it was okay.
That's how comfortable it was to be with Dwight.

The night was cold and windy, but not so bitter that
we had to hurry, and we strolled home over the squeaky
snow hand in hand. Lilac season at Kew be damned.
Next time I'd find an excuse to take my mitten off. I
really began to feel that there might be a next time.

"The moon is full," I suggested. But Dwight, being
neither romantic nor werewolf, did not fall upon me at
the news.

"Yes, it is," he agreed in his pure, earnest way.

We didn't say much after that. We picked our way
through the snow of the driveway, drawing nearer and
nearer the back doorstep, where one got kissed or, as
the case might be, didn't. Would he? Would there ever
be a better night? I was too tense to speak. Sometimes I
climbed up a step to be at kissing level with the boys
who walked me home, but Dwight and I were about the
same size. At the steps we paused, I with my back to
the door, Dwight facing me. He still held my hand.

"Well, it was a good game," he said.

"Yes, it was," I said. Lying. I hadn't watched the game. Good phrenological bumps, Dwight.

"Even if we didn't win," he added.

"Yes."

"I didn't know how we'd do, but we played pretty well. It was close."

"Close games are more exciting," I ventured. (Play close games with me, Dwight!)

"Too bad we lost, though."

"Yes. That *was* too bad."

There came my father up the driveway. He'd been at the game too. I dug my gradually freezing toes into the doorstep. I wasn't going in yet. Dwight dropped my hand.

"Hello there, Mr. Fisher," he called cheerfully.

"Hello, Dwight. What did you think of the game?" said my father.

"Good game, Mr. Fisher."

Dad went in. Dwight and I looked at each other. He seemed to have something on his mind.

"Good game!" I babbled. Was it contagious? Was this how birds felt, with nothing but "chickadeedeedee" to cover all ranges of courtship and emotion? Would we sing "goodgame" all night? Did I care? I'd sing it forever if this fool would just kiss me.

There was a silence. Dwight took my hands again, both of them. "Well," he said softly, "I guess I'd better go." The wind dropped and the stars were very still. He

lifted my hands, a little uncertainly, to his shoulders,
and I clasped them behind his neck.

"You might not believe this," he said, "but I'm really
kind of bashful."

I nodded mutely. I felt I'd been given a solemn gift
that I didn't know how to acknowledge. There seemed
to be no way to take that line of conversation further.

"Oh well," he said. "I guess we all have our faults."

"It's not a fault!" I cried, feeling that I'd failed him.
I needed to be older and wiser.

The world hung quiet on its axis for a moment while
he put his arms around me and touched my lips with his.
Their pressure was dry, warm, reassuring, a different
thing altogether from being kissed by random, randy
walkers-home. A civil convergence in love, not the Invasion of the Sucky Tongue that Slimed Chicago. I was
shaken by a new and happier response. Perhaps I should
count this as my first *real* kiss.

"Well, good night," he said, unclasping me.

"Good night," I whispered.

I knew, as I watched his retreating form, that I wasn't
going to write about this, or if I did I wasn't going to
hype it up, throw in flowers and butterflies and witty
conversation. Real life, right here at the back door beside
the trash can, here in the scouring drifts, here with nervous chattering of basketball, was enough. The gods vis-
ited even people like me.

I floated through the back door, not sure whether I
didn't feel the floor because I was walking on air or

because my feet were numb. I wasn't eager to talk, but I was too high to be cranky.

"Good game?" my mother asked, grinning.

"Yeah," I said.

"Know who won?"

I wanted to crow "I did" and she'd have loved that, but I couldn't, it was too private.

"I guess the other guys did," I said, remembering not the game but Dwight's conversation. She smiled yet more broadly.

"I was going to bring you an extra muffler pretty soon," she said. How did a straight kid like me get such a wise-ass mother?

As soon as I could, I went up to my room. No need to steel-wool my teeth this time. I'd never forget the date, but I wanted to write it down and look at it. January 10, 1958. I sat and smiled to myself and knew then what I wished I'd said to Dwight. I wished I'd said, "You certainly *are* bashful; I thought you'd *never* kiss me!"

Did that mean that already I was older and wiser?

CHAPTER ELEVEN

Dwight's amazing kiss did not lead to any further revelations in the week of anxiety that followed. Indeed, he had never seemed farther from me. By the light of that one kiss I tried to penetrate the murk of subsequent goings on and make sense of them. Dwight seemed almost to be avoiding me, to find reasons to leave a room when I came in.

Was he sorry he'd opened up as much as he had?

Was I, myself, a crummy kisser?

Had I failed him by having no reply to his admission of shyness?

Was this odd week a further manifestation of that shyness?

Had he turned to somebody else?

Had I done something wrong—(1) been too forward? (2) been too backward?

Worst, there was a kind of superstition current among us that a boy could tell how you felt about him from kissing you. If he had really found that out, my intensity might have scared him away. Conversely, not knowing the secret language of the lips, I might have sent some misleading signal—perhaps my tissues had told his that I did *not* love him. How could I tell? It was beyond me, the whole complicated thing, and I couldn't see a thing to do but be as nice as I could and wait.

I spent the week in misgivings and daydreamings, hair-triggered to give Dwight pieces of my notebook paper for his assignments, pass in his essays, snatch his dropped pencils from the floor. But I had some hope for Friday, for once again there was a basketball game and perhaps, given the same circumstances, the magic would repeat itself. Maybe he had just been preoccupied with getting ads for the yearbook. We'd see.

Friday morning I woke up filled with a kind of tentative good cheer, and I dressed with particular care in my straight gray-and-brown plaid skirt (my parents said it looked like a horse blanket, but it was fashionable) and a light gray crewneck sweater. I planned to be ready if fortune favored me. The sky was wearing gray as well, but I ignored it. Dwight's kiss still gave me hope. The school paper was coming out and I'd done the cover (giant snowflakes), and surely, surely, that basketball game would prove lucky.

By the end of morning chapel, when we sang "Just a Closer Walk with Thee," I felt in love not only with

Dwight but with the entire student body and the faculty
as well. I could probably have flown upstairs under my
own power, but I didn't like to be different. "Thee,"
I'm afraid, had stopped being God and started being
Dwight, ambling upstairs in his new Pendleton shirt.
How could a somewhat melancholy song so contribute
to my happiness? "When this feeble life is o'er/ Time
for me will be no more . . . ." But this feeble life was
prospering, thank you, and for now I had time, lots of
it. Time to straighten things out with Dwight, time to fill
my hope chest, time to grow and change and learn.

Love attacks have their disadvantages. I spent most of
the day fighting down impulses. The impulse to kiss
Dwight's tired-looking eyes in Solid Geometry. The impulse to turn around and study him in study hall. The
impulse to tell the truth in my French essay about what
I hoped to accomplish by the age of thirty years. I was
saved from that indiscretion only by not being able to
remember whether the verb for marrying was reflexive.
I distracted myself for a while by memorizing "Stone
Walls do Not a Prison Make" for future consolation
when things got trappy at home. I also spent some time
writing Dwight's name on a secret page in my notebook
that had previously been devoted to writing variations of
"Louisa Fisher PH.D., Dr. L. Fisher." It was not one
of your faster days.

After school I stopped by the dorm to pick up the
senior picture that Sabra had for me and retired to the

privacy of my room to read what she'd written on it. If
you really liked a person, you wrote on the back of the
photo real pledges of gratitude and affection, not just the
casual "It's been good going to school with you, A.F.A.
Clyde" that you got on the open folder. Sabra's remarks
were gratifying in the extreme, and I lingered to pop her
photo into a new frame, so the edges wouldn't curl. Out
my east window I saw Dwight and three other boys come
out of the restaurant and climb into a waiting car. He
was wearing a leather jacket and eating a hamburger,
and I thanked God briefly that he had these pleasures,
as well as adding a petition that he be back in time for
the basketball game. I did not ask for any particular
developments. If my religion was slightly offhanded in
this period of intense worldly distractions, at least I knew
the etiquette.

And speaking of God, I had promised my mother to
help set up tables for a church supper that night, so I
rode down with her and began to sort out plates—a pile
with clovers, a pile with wheat, a plain pile, a pile of
odds and ends. The church was freezing cold, the dank-
ness of my bedroom with an exponent of 100, and the
cheap silverware numbed my fingers. The china was
better handled with gloves. Unless the furnace picked up
more swiftly than I expected, this would be like eating
Jello salad in a tomb. Not that I expected to eat much,
what with nervousness about the basketball game and
Dwight. After a while my mother asked if I'd mind walking home and getting her a sweater, and I was glad of
the chance to get out. I didn't hurry much.

I noticed as I walked home that last week's snow was gone except for a few grubby patches beside the road. The road itself looked slick, and ice was beginning to skin over the puddles. But there, to my joy, was Viv, coming out of the restaurant.

"What are you doing here?" I asked, delighted.

"What are you doing yourself?" she snapped.

"I live here," I said, not at all out of humor. "Can't your father come, or what?"

"He's going to be pretty late," she said. "Bad roads."

"You might as well keep me company at the church supper, then," I said, "and we can go to the basketball game afterwards."

When she agreed, my spirits went up about fifty degrees. Dinner would be tolerable after all, and I thought it lucky to repeat as many circumstances as possible of last week's game. Viv had been beside me at that.

Of course I was impatient through dinner anyway, but Viv's companionship made it possible to slip out early. We got a ride with the principal's son Jimmy, whom we liked. His car slid back and forth across the street.

"I *told* you he was a wild driver," I said to Viv.

Jimmy grinned, flattered.

"There's Marc," said Viv. "I thought he was out sick today. I guess there's no cure like 3:15."

We laughed at this.

We were to stop by Viv's room first, and afterwards we'd go to my house so I could get ready—brush my

hair, put on fresh lipstick, change to my newer, darker
gray sweater. In the dorm, a freshman girl was crying
on the first floor landing.

"What ails her?" I whispered to Viv when we were
past her.

"She and her roommate were going to split up; I guess
they've done it," she said.

I sat on Sabra's bed while Viv brushed her hair. Someone else ran past the room in tears.

"My gosh," I said, "it sure is *wet* here tonight."

"I think she's been fighting with her boyfriend," said
Viv.

When the third girl we saw was also crying, Viv and
I began to giggle. We couldn't help it. But the third girl
was a friend, so we felt obliged to follow her and ask
what was wrong.

Her reply jerked us around a major corner in our lives
and left us gasping on the other side: "Spence and them
were in an accident, and Dwight Brown was killed."

I found that I had sat down rather suddenly on the
corner of her bed. I wasn't sure what had happened to
Viv, though I remembered her crying out and putting
her hands over her face; I was sucked into darkness like
quicksand and fighting for air. I have since heard others
speak of the shortness of breath that accompanies, like
a foreshadowing of your own end, the first news that

some beloved contemporary has died. I felt that, and the hot, heavy hand that seems to press you down—Atropos, Nemesis, Pluto. Somewhere something is jeering: you thought you were immune? And you lie, "No no, I didn't, let me up!" It's a lie because you never *really* knew. Some time passed.

"Come on, Fish, we'll go downstairs," Viv said. She sounded about fifty years old. We two were dry and despairing amid the showers of tears around us. We sat on the couch in the girls' lounge, and people came in and out and some stayed, but nobody turned on the lights. When we had heard the news repeated too often, seen too many girls collapse into corners or up against walls, sobbing, stared too long at the black window, we went outdoors.

It was not better there, only colder and windier. We met some boys who knew details; details were not comforting. Dwight had died while we sat at that dull supper, planning for things that wouldn't happen. Who would have guessed that people broke so easily? Viv was comforting, though. She was as stalwart and tactful and patient as if I'd ever confessed to her how I felt. Too bad I didn't know what I wanted or where I wanted to go, for Viv would have managed it somehow, but all things were alike indifferent. We looked at our watches. It was seven-thirty. Only seven-thirty! That meant we had a lot of night to get through, as well as a lot of life left to be endured. There was one desolate moment when Mrs.

Judson came into the dorm to get a candy bar for her youngest child, who was upset and couldn't sleep; we saw too clearly the ineffectiveness of a candy bar ever to fix the states of mind we'd grown into now.

We spotted Marc in the restaurant, on one of our prowls past. "Do you want to go in?" Viv asked.

"Okay," I said, "I don't care." And we found ourselves with Marc in the booth where only weeks ago we'd sat with Dwight and Sabra and Jewell. Marc's face, never expressive, had gone blank as stone. I watched his long fingers play with his coffee cup. After a while some younger kids came in. "Who's got change for a quarter?" one girl kept yelling. I thought, "If she plays 'Special Angel' that's it, I'll die. So much for the stiff upper lip," but nobody, not even the owner, gave her change. We left right after that.

"I really had change," I said.

"So did I," said Viv and Marc.

We walked up and down that empty street in that empty town and thought about the empty world. We said things like, "It doesn't seem possible" and "It's so hard to believe" and "Dwight of all people!" I guess mourners have said things like that for a thousand years— "Dwyght, of alle peple"—and it's probably never helped. Certainly it didn't help us.

"It will be bad Monday," said Marc at last.

"And Tuesday," I added dismally.

"It'll be bad for a long time and we'd just better get used to it," said Viv.

Forever, I thought. Bad forever.

All evening we wandered and grouped and regrouped and separated again, blundering together for comfort, not finding much. But we couldn't think of anything better. We looked at each other's sad eyes and straight faces and found nothing there but a blank grief to match our own. In the end we went back to the restaurant.

"Fish," said Viv, "I think you should go home. You have to go sometime."

"I don't want to," I said. "My mother will say something." Not even I knew what I meant by "something," but my wound was raw and private and I couldn't bear for a kind adult word to touch it. Our shock would be old news to them. This was not their affair.

"Want me to go talk to her?" she said. I nodded and she did.

Dear Viv, I've never known what she said, but my mother, when I came home, never made a sign that this wasn't an ordinary night, except that she didn't joke.

I felt then that a piece of me had left home already. And I knew, further, that some day I'd really go away. Because everyone does.

CHAPTER TWELVE

Dwight's death brought a hundred new experiences, mostly horrible, in its train. For instance, getting up the next morning, putting my feet on the icy floor and standing up to face a day empty of possibility. Downstairs there would be sneaky glances of concern, the newspaper headlines, announcements on the morning news, the unthinkable effort of eating a piece of toast so I'd qualify as healthy and be permitted to go out, out, to walk the road. It was a different world from the one I'd waked up to yesterday.

At the end of my driveway, at mid morning, I found Willard Jewell, who had hitchhiked back to school as soon as he'd heard. He had on a pair of dress shoes that I'd never seen on him before, and a topcoat. His feet had blistered on the way. He had no jokes to make, and if Viv had sounded fifty, he looked about sixty-five with his white face and red eyes. He poked at a pile of dirty snow with the toe of his black shoe.

"Well," he said finally, "Dwight's gone and there's nothing we can say will bring him back."

I nodded. Jewell and I, both in our own ways addicted to language, had run out of puns and metaphors.

What can be said about such a day? It was long, it hurt, and as we had done the night before, those of us left in town paced and sought comfort in odd places. For a while I went to the dorm and helped some other girls paint the faculty lounge, but I couldn't keep my mind on it. The teachers sang and danced up and down the corridor, a bizarre and touching effort to cheer us up, but who could get interested? Once after dark I walked past the restaurant and saw Dwight, clear as day, standing and playing the pinball machine, wearing his Pendleton shirt. Nobody had told me I'd hallucinate. But yes, by all means, better a mirage than nothing, though it was too keen a reminder of what I'd never really see. And as Jewell remarked later, there was nothing we could talk about that didn't remind us of Dwight, who had been part of everything.

I was desperate to go to the funeral, to see the last moment of the last bit of Dwight, and rather to my dulled

surprise my father agreed to drive me down to it, seven-
ty-five miles away in a little town on the coast. I would
have preferred to go with my friends, but I was in no
position to argue.

The coast doesn't get as much snow as the rest of the
state, but in winter it's gray and frozen and windy. It
doesn't look like a place where resurrection is possible.
I didn't say much on the way down, I guess, just stared
into the black-and-white lap of my best Jonathan Logan
dress, thankful I hadn't bought red. I'd even cut the bow
off the neck to make it plainer. All the same I couldn't
help taking some interest in where Dwight had come
from, a place made sacred by his retroactive presence.
And I would get a peep at his family, perhaps. I stared
at every cemetery we passed. Was that the one where
Dwight would lie? Was it good enough for him? Could
I, older and mobile, find it again and bring flowers?

The church was almost full when we got there. This
episode of pain had nearly started without me. My father
sat in the back and let me go down front to find a space
beside friends, but there was no room with Viv and Sabra, so I sat beside some other people I knew and stared
at the bank of flowers. And yes, briefly at Dwight, who
lay there like a grotesque centerpiece: the open coffin
had been draped with pink gauze to soften the stitched-
together puzzle of his face, but all it blurred was his
identity. He looked very flat and serious. His sparkle
had gone to wherever sparkles go.

My mind was so crowded with horror and impossibility that I heard only bits of what the minister was telling us. "I am the resurrection and the life." "Though he were dead, yet shall he live." "In my father's house are many mansions." Once I came out of my chaos to hear him saying, "Mourning is only a deeper form of love." "But it's a bad one," I wanted to say; "It hurts." We seemed to be there for quite a while, the yellow light from the stained glass making all of us look nearly as unreal as Dwight, and I put most of my energy into holding myself together. Black, lunatic rhymes ran though my head—Dwight, Dwight, endless night. Once I found myself thinking that whatever cowboys liked, they didn't like being dead.

I watched the boys, too sad to lift their feet, drag past the coffin when their turns came. I myself intended to get a long last look, to be bold and take away an eyeful of Dwight to last out my life, but I saw the scars first and turned my face away and then my time was past.

We came out of church into a kind of vacuum. Emptiness is extra big on the coast, with the whole ocean out there. But Jewell came and led me to the car where Viv and Sabra were. It was the only time I ever saw Sabra cry.

The cemetery was none of those I'd seen on the way in, but a desolation of puckerbrush and wind, with the garish green of a grass rug and a hole, an ordinary hole, in the earth. My Dwight in that? No comfort there. After

the briefest of blessings a little man sent us away, and
we heard a voice behind us say, "Lower." (As long as
you don't hear the clods dropping on the coffin, Scarlett,
folks aren't actually dead to you.)

My father most surprisingly sensed my need and let
me ride home with my friends, while he did the long and
dreary drive by himself, a piece of generosity for which
I, in my self-absorption, was not even grateful. Jimmy
Judson drove the car we rode in. I had known him all
our lives, but today he seemed someone new and older.
I was glad he was there.

Before the first frenzy of grief had faded into the long
ache of recovery, I went back to my typewriter and put
down everything I could remember. My family now let
me stay alone as much as I liked. I was desperate in those
first days for some scrap, some touch, some memento of
Dwight. I drew a little pencil sketch of him, wearing the
clothes he'd worn on his last day, and put it in a frame
in the bottom of a drawer. Every day when I got home
from school I opened the drawer and said hello to him.
I'd have liked to wear the gold pin, but I couldn't risk
its loss.

But memory isn't enough, when hope is gone. I was
plagued by the thought of all that Dwight and I would
never do, both amorous and otherwise, and so at last I
thrust Lucilla Shark into bed with Brownell Flite and

achieved a kind of paper consummation, necessarily vague about technical details, but tender. For a whole week I read it every day and it consoled me a little for what I foresaw as a lifetime of lonely polar sheets, for with whom else but Dwight would such closeness be thinkable? What those pages said was too private ever to tell.

At the end of that week I realized that no place was safe enough to hide that piece of intimacy, except my memory, so one evening when I was home alone I crept to the wood stove and burned the love scene, and the rest of the manuscript after it. The pages curled and blackened and fell to nothing while I watched, not rescued from annihilation's wake after all. My imaginary life with Dwight, like my real one, crumbled and drifted away.

CHAPTER THIRTEEN

Exactly five weeks and four days after Dwight died, I broke down and let Marc Andover kiss me, half way up the drive, in the middle of a snowstorm. I had seriously meant never to let anybody kiss me again, to have Dwight the last person who ever did it, and indeed I had fended off quite a few attempts in those thirty-nine days. But I finally wore down; I didn't have much spunk that winter.

That was a long winter, 1958, and a dreary one. I never went to any more basketball games, for somehow I didn't like being in the gym anymore, and in rural Maine in the winter, basketball is all there is for entertainment. I read a lot, as I always had, but only gloomy stuff suited me. I read *On The Beach*, about people dying of radiation poisoning, and I read all of "In Memoriam," Tennyson's long poem about grieving for his best friend. I copied most of it out on my typewriter, and when I came to an "Arthur" I'd stick in a "Dwight B" instead, because that made two syllables, but it never scanned very well. Like everything else, it seemed out of step. I did my homework. I tried to get interested in the imminence of college. I watched a little TV, but there seemed to be a lot of car wrecks on it. And every day I made an excuse to go upstairs as soon as I got home, and looked at my drawing of Dwight.

Willard Jewell began to come around too, that winter. We'd sit on the sofa to watch television and hold one another and talk a little now and then. I assumed at first that we were clinging together out of grief. I found this comforting. When certain moves of Willard's suggested that grief was not his principal impetus, I went on with it anyway. I liked old Jewell just fine, and sometimes he made me laugh a little. Besides, once I'd messed up on keeping my lips sacred to Dwight's memory, what else was left to lose?

The obvious answer to that didn't occur to me, perhaps because I regarded my virginity as a permanent, natural state, like being 5'2''. One afternoon early in May, when nature was beginning to show that some things come back, Willard and I found ourselves in the house after school, with several hours at our disposal. We necked for a while in silence, a depressed, dozy, lethargic silence on my part. Perhaps a thoughtful one on Jewell's, I don't know.

When he tipped me over and bore me down onto the

couch I was vaguely taken with the novelty of it, though not very comfortable.

"Easy, Jewell," I said after a few minutes of absent-minded grappling. "You're squashing my leg."

"Don't call me that; call me Willard," he said, suddenly serious. I remembered his sober and bereft face the morning after Dwight died, and I loved him a little.

"Off my leg, Willard," I said. He shifted his weight. I gave him an encouraging pat on the back. We lay still, side by side, for a moment.

"Up," he murmured at last and struggled to sit straight, pulling me up and against his shoulder. I waited passively.

We sat for what seemed a long time while Willard looked pensive and stroked my arm. I found the effect of this hypnotically soothing. Once when I was little my mother had shown me how she could mesmerize a chicken—she'd just grabbed a young one and flopped him down on the barn floor and stroked his neck until he lolled there by himself looking silly and dazed. I felt like that. The idea of my mother (and, via the medium of chickens, my father) was faintly, but not very, disturbing. I was glassy eyed.

"Fish," Willard said at last, "perhaps it's time you came to terms with the Life Force, Old Mother Nature, rape, riot, and revolution."

I was thinking dreamily that I didn't have the energy for revolution when he turned and looked me in the eye.

"Life goes on," he said.

"You need to snap out of this," he said, "and commit yourself to some course of action."

"Fish," he said, taking my hand, "it's spring. You and I are alive. We're seniors. Some college boy will get you next year. Let it be me, now. Let's make love before your folks get home; that's a course of action. Couldn't we go up to your room and be private?"

My room? That was private indeed. Dangerous too. When my friends and I were around nine or so, all our mothers had suddenly announced that children of opposite sexes could not play in one another's rooms any more, for dreadful things could happen. (What they were, a friend with older sisters told me in one terse, four-letter word. It was hard for me to imagine the unspeakable being done to me by some third-grade friend I'd known all my life, but who can penetrate the mysteries of human behavior?) The dangers seemed remote, though, and not very important. "The *grave's* a fine and private place" came into my head, and then I didn't seem to care anymore what happened. I worked up a kind of dopey politeness.

"Certainly. Come along," I said.

It took effort to lift one foot ahead of the other as we went up the stairs. I didn't feel alarmed, just unreal. Willard looked nervous and once he actually took my elbow. That struck me funny.

Still locked into politeness, I found myself trying to give Willard a tour of the family photos we passed going down the hall to my room. I was just showing him the picture of my maternal grandparents' farm when I saw how ridiculous this was. He was being as mannerly as a guest could be, but he didn't look happy.

"Never mind," I said. "My room's down here."

I took his hand and led him into it, feeling in spite of the circumstances my familiar pride in how nice it looked. Except perhaps for the bed, which looked about an acre across and eight feet high. Had it always taken up that much of the room? We marched across the floor and hoisted ourselves onto its edge, where we sat side by side for a bit.

"Do we have to do this with Viv and Sabra staring at us?" he asked, nodding towards the pictures on my bookcase.

"I guess we could turn them around," I said slowly. But I was remembering another picture, drawn in pencil and tucked into a bottom drawer. My poor facsimile of Dwight was with us too. No shutting those eyes behind wood. Being now passed beyond the physical, his eye like God's was always upon me. Thou Dwight seest me. Perhaps he'd understand that I did it out of grief and desperation.

"Well," said Willard.

"Well," I said, and we rolled over onto the bed-spread.

But it didn't work, somehow. When we lay against each other, none of our superficial bumps and hollows fitted any more. Our hands didn't meet. Our feet kicked each other by accident. Both lust and lethargy were passing away. Lethargy anyway. Little or none of the lust had been mine in the first place, but I sensed that Willard too was finding the situation eroded.

"Willard," I said, sitting up, "I think I just can't do this after all. I'm sorry."

He sat up too. "I hear," he said, "that it isn't too great the first time anyway."

I kissed him then with real affection, for being himself and a part of my life. For not waving his pistols and insisting on being a cowboy. For being my friend instead. I had never loved him more.

We sat on the edge of the bed again, shoulder to shoulder, and it felt natural. This room was the place where I took my friends, and Willard was my friend. I was within an inch of offering to show him my jewelry.

We looked together out my east windows, where Venice and Paris lay beyond our sight, once again desirable.

"Willard," I said, feeling new freedom, "can I ask you something?"

"What is it?" he said.

I only blushed a little. "What *do* cowboys like?" I said. He was my friend now for sure; it was safe to ask.

Willard looked startled, even alarmed, but he pulled himself together. "Why," he said, "we almost did it."

I looked out my window and smiled to myself.

"No," I said, "no, I think they prefer the wide open ranges."

CHAPTER FOURTEEN
Epilogue

What can I tell you? We all got on with our lives. That's a more or less involuntary activity. Some of us went to college, some of us didn't. Some of us married once or twice, some of us stayed single. Viv's a school principal herself now, and since she divorced that not very satisfactory man she had earlier dated at Canterbury, she's raised two sons single-handedly, with lots of firmness and efficiency and love. Sabra married a lawyer, had her babies with a minimum of labor, owns a house with a swimming pool and a tennis court, and stays thin; her magic has held. Willard's a tour bus driver, he really is, and I often think how his passengers must adore him. We've lost touch with Marc.

Me, I've been to Istanbul. Been to the Harvard Museum, too, and once I actually went down to Kew in lilac time. I didn't wander hand in hand with love, though. I wandered with my mother, who sometimes traveled with me after my father died, and that day a sudden cloudburst nearly drowned us and the lilacs too. But yes, I remembered my Senior English anthology, and I thought about Dwight, though there are days when I don't.

The idea that time heals your wounds isn't quite right. Time doesn't heal them as much as it moves them a little farther back in your head, where you don't bump into them every minute and set them bleeding. They're still wounds.

But although the grief doesn't go away, it gets more secret. The incident turns into a kind of underground, central myth in your personality, until you're surprised and a little shocked to hear the dead person's name mentioned, as though someone had been reading your private mail. Twenty-five years after Dwight died I had lunch with a couple of friends, one of whom had taught at Canterbury while we were there. "You remember Dwight Brown," she said.

"Come on, lady," I managed not to say, "my whole life has been a remembering of Dwight Brown."

"Of course," I said instead, or maybe I just nodded. Do I remember God? Do I remember the Easter Bunny? Has every character who dies young in books been Dwight to me for what seems like forever?

"He was so smart," she said. "He'd have been valedictorian if he'd lived."

For just an instant I opened my mouth to protest—no, no, it was always going to be me, you fool—and then I shut it again. I've had a chance to do other things.

"Yes, he would have," I said. A small bouquet for you, Dwight, buddy.

Then there are the dreams. The earliest ones were awful, blood and open graves and once Dwight's head in a box. Nowadays they're rare but often faintly erotic, and I wake up with the precise feel of the back of his head in my hand, or see some forgotten detail of his skin, or remember how exactly the right height we were for kissing each other. I always know in the dreams that he's dead, really, but it doesn't make any difference—not a handicap that you'd hold against someone you love.

Canterbury's gone now, sold to a Bible college, and we're scattered, and other people live in my parents' house, but sometimes it all comes back. Only a little while ago I had quite an elaborate dream about Dwight and all of us. We'd triumphed over Mr. Judson in some sort of permission-getting political ploy, and were very full of ourselves. We were lolling about in triumph on the front campus, picnicking, and Dwight was lying beside me. But then some rational part of my brain took over and time jarred back into place. I looked around and saw that we were just a bunch of middle-aged revelers on a Bible school lawn, and that we'd left Dwight behind.